TAKE TIME
TO READ

# Creamy Casserole Murder

## Book Fifteen in the Darling Deli Series

## By

Pa

# Copyright 2016 Summer Prescott Books

**Author's Note:** On the next page, you'll find out how to access all of my books easily, as well as locate books by best-selling author, Summer Prescott. I'd love to hear your thoughts on my books, the storylines, and anything else that you'd like to comment on – reader feedback is very important to me. Please see the following page for my publisher's contact information. If you'd like to be on her list of "folks to contact" with updates, release and sales notifications, etc…just shoot her an email and let her know. Thanks for reading!

Also…

…if you're looking for more great reads, from me and Summer, check out the Summer Prescott Publishing Book Catalog:

http://summerprescottbooks.com/book-catalog/ for some truly delicious stories.

**Contact Info for Summer Prescott Publishing:**

Twitter: @summerprescott1

Blog and Book Catalog: http://summerprescottbooks.com

Email: summer.prescott.cozies@gmail.com

And…look up The Summer Prescott Fan Page on Facebook – let's be friends!


If you're an author and are interested in publishing with Summer Prescott Books – please send Summer an email and she'll send you submission guidelines.

# TABLE OF CONTENTS

# CREAMY CASSEROLE

# MURDER

**Book Fifteen in the Darling Deli Series**

# CHAPTER ONE

*It's good to be back*, Moira Darling thought when she woke up in her own bed the first morning after returning from her cruise in the Caribbean. The trip had been an experience that she wouldn't soon forget, especially the beautiful scenery and summer-like weather, but nothing could compare to home.

Maverick, her loyal German shepherd, perked his head up as she stretched. Keeva, the giant Irish wolfhound that she had taken in a few months ago, was already up, her large head resting on the bed near Moira's pillow. Both dogs looked thrilled to see her finally awake, and she couldn't blame them—it was past ten in the morning already.

*Yesterday must have really taken it out of me*, she thought. She and Candice, her twenty-one-year-old daughter, had disembarked the cruise ship in the early afternoon, then had rushed to the airport to make their flight back to Michigan. It had been close, but they had managed to get on the plane at the last second, and just a few hours later, David had picked them both up at the airport in Traverse City.

The dogs had nearly bowled her over when she got home last night, and both of them still seemed to be unusually clingy. She felt bad for having been gone from them for so long, but at least she knew David had taken spectacular care of them. If there was anyone she trusted to watch her dogs, it was him.

"All right, all right, I'm getting up," she told the two impatient pooches. She was supposed to be at the deli in just a couple of hours, and the list of stuff she wanted to get done first seemed endless. Whether she was ready or not, her day had to begin.

She went downstairs, let the dogs out into the back yard, started the coffee machine, then turned her attention to the suitcases sitting by the front door. Last night she had been too tired even to begin the task of unpacking, but there wasn't any putting it off now. With a longing glance at the still gurgling coffee machine, she got to work.

David had stayed at her house for the duration of her stay on the cruise, and he had left it in stellar shape. The floors had been swept and mopped, the kitchen was spotless, and even the dogs' yard had been cleaned. *He's definitely a once-in-a-lifetime sort of man,* she thought as she finished loading the last of her laundry into the washing machine in the mudroom, which had also been swept out and mopped. *I think the house is even cleaner than it was when I left.* She felt a bit bad that he had done so much without asking for anything in return. She had been hesitant to even ask him to watch the dogs, knowing how busy he was.

*He definitely went above and beyond,* she thought with a smile, watching the clothes begin to spin in the washer. *I'll have to think of some way to repay him.* She would have to figure all of that out later, though. Right now she had to get dressed for work, then go and see how Darling's DELIcious Delights had fared without her.

An hour later, she pulled into the deli's parking lot in her green SUV. The dogs had looked heartbroken when she left, but she had promised them that she would be back that evening—no more trips for her, at least not for the foreseeable future.

The deli looked the same as it always had... except for the big banner hanging over the front door that read *Welcome Home, Ms. D!* She grinned at the sight of it and happy tears moistened her cheeks. She hadn't expected anything like this and was reminded once again of why she loved her job so much.

Darrin and Allison were waiting for her inside, both smiling in welcome as she walked through the door. She looked around, impressed to see how clean the deli was. It smelled amazing too; the little blackboard on the counter declared that the soup of the day was southern corn chowder, and her stomach growled at the thought of the sweet, filling, slightly spicy soup simmering away in the kitchen. She would definitely have to get herself a bowl of it before settling in to work.

"Welcome back, Ms. D," Allison said. "How was your trip?"

"It was…" She paused, not wanting to wreck the happy return with stories of the events of the competition, which had been cut short due to a murder. "Well, the cruise ship was very nice, and the ocean and islands were just beautiful. I'll tell you more about it later. How did things go here?"

"Everything was fine here, though we did get a few catering requests that I left for you to look at, since I wasn't sure how busy you'd be after getting back," Darrin told her. "But as far as day-to-day things, everything went off without a hitch. A lot of the customers asked after you when they didn't see you, and I'm sure a lot of people will be stopping in to say hi now that you're back."

Moira smiled at that. One of her favorite things about running the deli was the personal connection with her customers. In a town as small as Maple Creek, especially in the off-season for tourists, she recognized almost every person that stopped at the deli, and they all knew her, too. It would be nice to see all of her regulars again, though she was sure talking about the cruise would begin to get old after a while.

That reminded her…

"I have pictures of the trip on my tablet if you want to see," she told them. "I thought I would make a sort of a slideshow so people who ask about my trip will have a chance to look through them."

Showing people pictures of her trip turned out to be a good idea. It saved her a lot of time when one of her customers wanted to know how the cruise had gone, and everyone seemed to love the gorgeous photos. By the time five o'clock rolled around and people began getting out of work, business was booming. She had just finished serving a roasted chicken breast sandwich to an elderly man who had been especially interested in the pictures of the cruise, since he was thinking of surprising his wife with one for their anniversary, when two of her closest friends walked in.

"It's great to see you," she told Martha and Denise when they approached the register. "I was hoping to get together sometime this week—I have so much to tell you, but I can't do it here."

"Will you be able to make our normal Wednesday morning coffee?" Martha asked. "We can get a corner table. As long as it isn't too busy, we should be able to talk pretty privately."

"Sure," the deli owner said. "I gave myself a light schedule this week while I get back into the swing of things, so that works for me if you both can make it."

"Even though the Grill opens earlier now, mornings still aren't a particularly busy time," Denise said. "So that works for me, too. In the meantime, you've *got* to tell us how the cruise was."

It was wonderful to get caught up with her friends, though once she mentioned some of what had happened on the cruise ship, they were dying to know more. She felt bad making them wait until Wednesday for the full story, but she was reluctant to get into details with so many customers around. The last thing she needed was more rumors being spread about her and the trouble she kept getting herself into. The deli was doing really well now; she didn't need any bad publicity to wreck that. As her friends left, each with a small to-go bowl of corn chowder, she swore she would go into more detail later. They wouldn't be disappointed, she knew. The cruise had been many things, but boring was not one of them.

Despite the busy day, she felt overwhelmingly good to be back. It was wonderful to work in the deli's kitchen again, which she knew like the back of her hand, to prepare the food for the next day's special, and it was even better to be able to take her time and cook stress-free. She hadn't liked cooking with a timer ticking away—the pressure had taken a lot of the fun out of making food for her. *Overall it was a good experience, though*, she thought as she scrubbed the counters at closing time. *I do feel that the competition made me more confident in what I do, and at least now I'll always be able to say that I've done it.*

After closing, Moira paused outside the deli and looked inside fondly. She had built so much, and continued to build so much, both at the deli and in her personal life. Her business was thriving and her relationship with David seemed to be going better than ever. Her life was as near to perfect as she could hope for. What could go wrong?

# CHAPTER TWO

"David's going to be here any minute, and I still can't find that other earring," Moira muttered, digging through her vanity drawer once again in hopes that she had somehow missed it the two other times she had done exactly the same thing. The earring, a small diamond stud that her father had gotten her decades before, had been missing for a while, and she suspected that Candice's cat Felix was to blame. She had watched the little beast for a week a while ago, and she was still finding bits of jewelry and socks that he had stashed away throughout the house.

One of her rings seemed to be missing as well, though she couldn't blame that one on the cat. She had worn it just a couple of days before leaving for the cruise. Where could it have gone? *I really need to reorganize my jewelry*, she thought. *I'm sure I wouldn't lose things as much if I actually had proper places to put it.* Her old jewelry boxes had all been destroyed in the house fire a few months back, and she hadn't gotten around to replacing them yet.

Deciding that it might be smartest to think like a cat, she got down on her hands and knees and began looking under the furniture in her bedroom. Under her nightstand, she found a lipstick that had disappeared around the same time as her earring—Felix had been busy—and knew she must be getting close. Sure enough, she found the piece of jewelry under her bed, way back against the wall. Her fingers closed on it just as a knock sounded below at the front door.

She managed to get the earring on without fumbling and gave herself a quick once-over in the mirror before hurrying downstairs. For their dinner date at the Redwood Grill, she played up her cruise-acquired tan by wearing a silver and pale green dress—not too dressy, but not too casual either. It would be the first time that she'd seen David since he had picked her up at the airport the other day, and she was feeling giddy at the prospect. She had missed him the most while she was gone, and no amount of video calls could beat actually seeing him in person.

"Come on in," she said when she opened the door, after greeting him with a kiss. "I've got to run to the ladies' room really quickly, then I'll be ready to go."

After freshening up, she stepped out of the bathroom and stroked Keeva's head—the dog had been waiting outside the bathroom door for her, having been reluctant to leave her side since she had returned—and walked into the living room expecting to find David and Maverick. Surprisingly, the room was empty.

"David?" she called, walking back out into the hallway toward the kitchen. He wasn't there, either. She was just about to check the backyard, thinking he might have gone outside with Maverick while he was waiting, when she heard footsteps coming down the stairs.

The private investigator reached the bottom of the stairs just as she did, and Maverick was close behind him. She thought she saw a flash of something like guilt across his face, but when she raised her eyebrows he just grinned at her and shrugged.

"Maverick must have heard a mouse or something," he said. "He raced up there after you went to the bathroom."

"I heard something skittering around in the attic the other day," she said with a sigh, adding yet another thing to her mental to-do list. "I'll have to take a peek up there sometime—but not right now. I'm ready to go if you are."

They said goodbye to the dogs and took their leave, Moira pausing to lock the front door behind them. She caught up with David slowly, still thinking about his mysterious behavior on the stairs. For some reason, she felt like he hadn't quite been honest with her.

The Redwood Grill was just as welcoming as ever, and despite having enjoyed all of the cruise ship's fancy restaurants, Moira was glad to be back on more familiar ground. The hostess recognized them and offered them their usual secluded booth in the back. The deli owner ordered a glass of chardonnay to begin with, and browsed through the menu, taking her time to look at the new options. Every few weeks, Denise, who owned the Grill, switched out some of their less popular options with brand new ones or old favorites, which kept their customers coming back to try new things. Moira loved the variety offered by the Redwood Grill: the choices ranged from Tex-Mex, to seafood, to sizzling cuts of expensive steaks. David usually opted for something with red meat, but she liked trying some of the different options, and whenever something new popped up on the menu she usually ordered it.

"I'll have the soybean casserole, please," she told the waiter when he showed up to take their order.

"And I'd like the surf and turf platter," David said. "Extra steak sauce, if you can."

"I'm glad we were both able to do this," Moira said once the waiter had left. "I've missed you. Video calling you from my tablet just wasn't quite good enough."

"I missed you, too," he admitted. "So did the dogs, of course. I think they were disappointed whenever I got back without you with me."

"I'm sure they weren't too sad," she replied, chuckling. "After all, they *did* get to go to work with you a couple times. That must have made up for it at least a bit. Thanks again for watching them, by the way."

"Oh, it was fun. They're good dogs, and hanging out together gave us all something to do while you were gone."

She smiled at him, thinking once again just how lucky she was to have met him. He seemed to be thinking the same thing, because he slid his hand across the table, wrapped his fingers around hers, and squeezed, smiling back at her.

"So, what are your plans for this week?" he asked.

"Rest, finish unpacking, and catch up with everything that's been going on around here since I left," she told him. "Then I'm going to start focusing on the deli more. We've been getting more catering requests than ever, so I've been thinking of expanding again, maybe hiring one or two new people to focus on the catering side of things. Being open seven days a week and nearly twelve hours a day is already a stretch for the team I have now, and adding catering to the mix just puts extra pressure on everyone."

"That sounds like a good idea," he said. "I have to say, I am extremely impressed with how much the deli has grown just since I've known you. You've really got a gift for this, Moira."

"It's something I enjoy," she said simply. "I don't know if I'm especially good at it, but I enjoy it enough to want to keep on going even when it gets tough. I just wish I hadn't waited so long to open up the deli. I feel like all of those other years were just a waste— other than raising Candice, of course."

"Who knows," he said. "Maybe if you had tried to start a business twenty years ago, it wouldn't have succeeded as well as the deli has. Besides, if you *had* started a business back then, you'd probably be so successful that you would have moved out of Maple Creek, and then I never would have met you."

"I love this town, so I don't think I'd leave even if I was a millionaire," she told him, grinning. "You might have been better off with someone else anyway, though. Most women don't have a near-death experience every time they step outdoors."

"Sometimes you have near-death experiences even when you're indoors," he pointed out.

"You're not helping," she said with a laugh.

"Your life might be slightly crazy at times," he admitted more seriously after chuckling with her for a moment. "But you're worth it. I don't want you to ever think otherwise."

She felt her face heat as he took her hand and kissed her fingers. It looked like romance wasn't dead, not even for someone of her age.

When David dropped her off at home later that evening she was still giddy with happiness. Everything about her life seemed perfect right then. She was dating an amazing man, her business was doing well, her daughter was happy and successful, and even her dogs were healthy and well-behaved. Things couldn't be better.

Smiling to herself, she went upstairs to her bedroom to take off her dress and change into something more comfortable for the evening. Reaching for the door to her jewelry cabinet to stash her earrings, she paused. Sitting in plain sight on top of the vanity was the ring she had been looking for earlier. *How on earth did I miss that?* she wondered, annoyed. She had spent so long looking for it, and it had been right in front of her the whole time. *I must be going crazy*, she thought. *Either that or those mice in the attic have been raiding my jewelry while I was gone.* That brought back thoughts of the probable rodent infestation that she would have to deal with, and she sighed. Tomorrow she would stop at the hardware store and get some live traps so she could relocate the little freeloaders. Tonight she was determined to relax, spend time with the dogs, and enjoy the peace and quiet for as long as she could.

# CHAPTER THREE

The peace and quiet only lasted until she sank into sleep a few hours later. Her dreams were filled with giant mice, an endless ocean made of soup, and something nameless and terrifying chasing her through the maze-like halls of an old ship. She woke up gasping, certain for a moment that she was still on the cruise ship, and only gradually realizing that she was actually at home in her own bedroom, with her two dogs sleeping loyally on the floor next to her bed.

"Keeva, Maverick, come on up, you guys," she said, patting the bed and sitting up to turn on the reading light on her nightstand. She didn't normally let the dogs sleep with her—they were so big that their panting shook the whole bed—but after a bad dream nothing helped more than some cuddle time with the pups.

The two dogs jumped eagerly on the bed, Maverick throwing himself down by her feet and the wolfhound laying down more delicately on the bed beside her. Moira tugged the blankets up and rested back against the pillow, still shaken by the dream and glad that she had the dogs to keep her company. She didn't know if she would be able to live out here so far from town all alone without them. *If you count the dogs, I haven't lived alone for over twenty years*, she thought as she reached over to turn off the light. *The house would feel so empty if I was the only one here.*

She settled back down in the darkness and closed her eyes, trying to fall back to sleep with the comforting warmth of the dogs pressed against her. She was just beginning to drift off when her phone went off, making her jump. Wincing at the loud noise, she sat up and grabbed the phone, her eyes resting on the glowing digits of the alarm clock just long enough to register the time. Three o'clock in the morning. Who could be calling her this early? Whoever it was, she was prepared to bet that they weren't calling with good news.

"Hello?" she said, wide awake now.

"Moira?" a familiar voice asked. It took her a moment to place it.

"Reggie?"

"I'm so glad you answered." The old man was speaking in a low voice—almost a whisper—and she had to turn the volume up on her phone to hear him. "You need to get over here right away."

"Why, Reggie? What happened? Why aren't you calling Eli?" She hoped that the young man was all right. Candice had started dating him a few months back, and they were inseparable now.

"Eli wouldn't know what to do," the grandfather whispered. "You will. I need your help. Someone's been murdered."

All of the air seemed to rush out of Moira.

"Murdered?" she managed. "At Misty Pines?"

The assisted-living home seemed like a peaceful place for the most part, and the staff seemed to truly care about the residents. She knew that if someone really had been killed, instead of passing quietly in their sleep as most residents did eventually, it would be the talk of the home for months.

"I heard it all happen in the room next to mine," he said. "I woke up and heard Beatrice shouting for help, then something muffled her yells... then she got quiet. Too quiet. A little bit later the paramedics showed up."

"You need to call the police, Reggie," she said. "They'll know how to handle this."

"The police were here," he said, his voice growing louder with his frustration. "I went out to tell them what I heard, but they didn't take me seriously. Alberta sent me back to my room with some more sleeping pills. I didn't take them." He said the last part smugly, as if he had pulled one over on the director of the assisted-living home. Moira smiled—she loved the old man's spirit.

"Did you take sleeping pills earlier in the evening, too?" she asked, her brain making a connection.

"I take sleeping pills every night. You try falling asleep without help at my age. There are far too many memories stuffed inside this old head to make sleep easy without the help of medication."

The deli owner frowned, thinking about everything the elderly man had told her. He had woken from a drug-induced sleep to hear another elderly resident making noises in her room, and she had later passed away. Though she wanted to give the man the benefit of the doubt, it didn't exactly sound like a clear-cut murder case to her. She liked Reggie a lot, but he did get confused sometimes. It would have been easy for him, still half-asleep with his brain muddled from the sleeping pills, to confuse his dreams with reality.

"Did you hear anyone in the room next door? Did they say anything?" she asked. "Anyone besides your friend Beatrice, that is?"

"No, not that I can remember, but I'm sure someone else was with her. The door to her room slammed shut a few minutes after she stopped shouting." He fell silent for long enough that Moira wondered if he had fallen asleep. Just as she was about to speak, he cleared his throat and added, "I know what you think, that I'm just some crazy old man, but I know what I heard. Beatrice was killed, and whoever did it is going to get away scot-free unless we do something about it."

She heaved a sigh, covering the phone with her hand so Reggie couldn't hear her frustration. It was true: her gut instinct was to dismiss his concerns, but that wasn't fair to him. *How horrible must it be,* she thought, *to be so powerless when you're so sure that something was wrong?* Because whether someone really had been killed or not, the old man obviously *believed* that it had happened. It was real to him, and that was what mattered.

"How about I come out tomorrow? I can't really do anything tonight anyway. Tomorrow I can take a look around, see if anyone is acting suspicious, and we can have lunch together. I'll even bring David, if he's free."

"Okay," Reggie said, sounding relieved. "I know that between the two of you you'll be able to figure out who did this. You won't let him get away with it. Thanks for believing me, Moira."

With that, the call was over. The deli owner returned her phone to her nightstand and stared sadly at her clock. So much for a good night's rest; she'd be lucky if she even managed another three hours before having to wake up. Her shift at the deli would only last a few hours, but it started early, and she had never been a morning person.

She managed to get back to sleep more quickly than she had thought she would. When she woke up, just before leaving her house, she sent a text to David, asking him if he could meet her at Misty Pines for lunch. She didn't tell him about the murder that Reggie claimed to have heard in the room next to his. She knew what his response would be; if there was once thing that the private investigator was a stickler about, it was her safety. If he thought there was even the slightest chance that someone really had been killed, then he would do everything in his power to keep her away from the assisted-living home, short of actually forbidding her to go.

In the daylight, the thought of Reggie actually being right about the murder seemed even more far-fetched. It wasn't that the old man was a liar... quite the opposite, in fact. But even if he had heard Beatrice shouting for help, that didn't mean someone had killed her. The woman might have awoken in pain and called out for help from a nurse. And the slamming of the door after she had fallen silent? Well that could have been one of the nurses rushing in to try to save her, or even the door to a different room completely slamming shut behind one of the residents. He hadn't heard any other voices, so if the paramedics and staff seemed unconcerned, then there probably wasn't anything to worry about. Hopefully she would be able to put Reggie's mind to rest, and that would be the end of it.

For the time being, she put thoughts of Reggie out of her mind. She had other things to focus on, namely, introducing a new item to the deli's sparse breakfast menu. During her cruise trip, she had come up with a recipe for a breakfast cookie similar to one of her grandmother's dishes. She had spent some of her extra time on the cruise scribbling ideas for tasty variations to the recipe on a pad of paper, and was eager to try them. With the deli's website already updating, promising free samples of the breakfast cookies to anyone who came in before eleven, the pressure was on. If the cookies were a hit, they could offer their early-rising guests something besides quiche and fruit, which would lead to more business, more publicity, and even more loyal customers—something the deli could never          have          enough          of.

# CHAPTER FOUR

"Are we all out of the cinnamon blueberry breakfast cookies, Ms. D?" Allison asked. Her blond hair was beginning to come out of her ponytail, and she looked hurried and tired. The deli had been booming with business all morning. Enough people had been drawn in with the promise of free food that Moira was tempted to do this every time they came up with a new dish to offer. *Though next time I have to make sure we have more people scheduled to work,* she thought, feeling bad for her haggard employee.

"I've got a new batch just about to go into the oven," she told the girl. "But this will be the last tray of them today. We should start reminding people that the free samples end at eleven."

"I'll be sure to tell people when they ring up their food." After trying a free sample, most people were buying more of the cookies, in addition to their usual quiche and coffee or juice.

"What type of cookie seems to be doing the best?" the deli owner asked, putting the tray into the oven, then leaning against the counter to take a breather.

"The peanut butter, banana, and chocolate chip ones, definitely," her employee said. They had made three varieties of cookie to begin with: the cinnamon blueberry; the peanut butter, banana, chocolate chip; and an especially gooey caramel apple cookie.

"That's not surprising," Moira said. "It's hard to beat that flavor combination. I'm glad that people seem to be enjoying the cookies—I'm really excited to start serving them." The peanut butter, banana, chocolate chip breakfast cookies were gooey and sweet, yet still managed to be at least somewhat healthy. Made with oats, they pulled apart easily and were best right out of the oven, though they were good even after they cooled. She had a feeling that they would soon be a favorite with any of her customers with a sweet tooth.

"Me too. I think they're delicious, and it will be nice to have something other than quiches to eat for breakfast when I come in early. Not that I don't love Dante's quiches, of course, but variety is the spice of life."

"Too true," the deli owner said. "That's one of the reasons I love this place. The possibilities for new food and new recipes are endless."

By the time her shift ended and Darrin and Meg had shown up to relieve her and Allison, David had texted her back. She smiled when she read his reply; he was free, and would be meeting her for lunch at Misty Pines in forty minutes. She would have just enough time to go home, shower quickly and change, and let the dogs out before driving over to the assisted-living home. She was glad for that; it would be nice to get out of her work clothes and freshen up before seeing the private investigator. Even though he had seen her covered in soot, mud, and blood, she still hated the thought of showing up to lunch sweaty and smelling of the deli's kitchen.

She ended up getting to Misty Pines a few minutes late, but David, who had waited outside for her, didn't mention it. Instead, he greeted her with a kiss. As they walked toward the assisted-living home's entranceway, he asked her how her day had gone.

"Good," she told him. "Though it was way busier than I expected. I felt bad for Allison—she ended up having to run back and forth from the kitchen to the register. I haven't written down a legible recipe for the others to follow yet, so I had to do all the cooking."

"The breakfast cookies were a success, then?" he asked. "I know you were excited about them on the cruise."

"Oh, yes. People loved them. I really wish that I had thought of them sooner, but it wasn't until I had to throw something together under pressure that I remembered my grandmother making them. That was years ago, of course, and I still don't think I have her recipe exactly right, but the cookies are good anyway."

"Knowing you, they're delicious." He grinned at her. "I'll try to stop in for breakfast sometime this week and try one. Sorry I couldn't make it today—I had an early meeting with a client."

"Oh, that's fine. I was stuck back in the kitchen the whole time, anyway. I really need to work on making a new recipe book for the deli." She sighed. "Just one more thing that I have to do."

"Why not have one of the employees do it?" he asked.

"Well, I'd still have to write out all of the recipes for them, which is the hard part. After that, it doesn't take too long to slip the pages into plastic sleeves and put them in a binder. Sorry… I shouldn't be talking about work right now. I want to focus."

David held the first set of doors open for her. She walked in and paused in front of the second set of doors, which automatically locked and required a code to open. *That's another reason I don't think what Reggie heard was a murder,* she thought. *The only people who have the codes to the doors are the staff and some of the more frequent visitors. A stranger wouldn't be able to get in in the middle of the night.* Hopefully Reggie would listen when she told him that she thought he had been wrong about Beatrice's death being a murder. The old man could be stubborn, and she had a worrisome feeling that this just might be one of those cases where he decided to stick to his guns.

A smiling aide punched in the code and unlocked the doors for them. When asked where Reggie was, she led them over to one of the small round tables in the dining room. Eli's grandfather was sitting alone, poking at his food. Looking up, he gave the couple a relieved smile.

"Thanks for coming," he said. "I was worried that you had forgotten. Let's hurry up and eat so you can start investigating."

David looked over at her with raised eyebrows, correctly suspecting that something was up. The deli owner blushed. She hadn't told him why she wanted to meet here for lunch, and he hadn't asked. He was fond of the old man too, and had probably just assumed that this was nothing more than a social visit.

"Reggie, why don't you tell David what you told me?" she said, pulling out a chair and taking a seat. "I think it's best that he hears it from you."

The elderly man launched into his tale, eagerly telling David everything that he had told Moira the night before. *He certainly seems to be pretty clear on what happened,* she thought. *I have no idea how I'm going to convince him that none of this is actually evidence of foul play. A woman died... but nothing points to someone killing her.*

"I think I even know who did it," the old man finished. The deli owner blinked.

"What?" she said.

"Well, after breakfast I spent the morning trying to figure out who had motive to kill poor Beatrice. She was a sweetheart, everyone liked her. But there is one person who would benefit from killing her, and that's her son."

"Why do you say that?" David asked. He seemed to be taking Reggie seriously, or at least giving him the benefit of the doubt.

"Because she was well off, and he wasn't," the elderly man replied. "He didn't even have money to buy a new car after his broke down—I heard him tell her that was why he takes the bus everywhere now."

"And she had him in her will?" the private investigator guessed. Reggie nodded, and David frowned. He caught Moira's eye and nodded toward the dining room door. "Reggie, will you excuse us? We'll be right back; I just want to bounce my ideas off of Moira without chancing anyone else listening in."

Reggie nodded, and Moira and David got up and left the dining room. The private investigator leaned against the wall outside the door, and the deli owner stood next to him.

"What do you think?" he asked.

"He seems pretty sure that there was some sort of foul play," she said with a sigh. "Look, I'm sorry. I should have told you why I wanted to meet here, but you get so weird about me being involved with this sort of thing."

"By 'weird,' I'm assuming you mean 'concerned for your safety'," he replied with a smile. "I admit that I can get a little overprotective sometimes, although to be fair, your track record for staying out of trouble isn't all that stellar. But in this case... I don't think you have anything to worry about. Reggie's a great guy who's concerned about the circumstances of his friend's death, but there really isn't any evidence that points to her being murdered."

"What about her son, though?" she asked. "If Reggie was right, then he really could have a motive to kill her."

"Without any other evidence, a motive isn't enough," he pointed out. "Look, if you really think that there's something to what Reggie is saying, I'll take a look around. Otherwise, let's just enjoy our lunch and do our best to convince him that Beatrice's death, though tragic, was a natural death."

"At first I didn't think there was anything to his story, but he just seems so sure..." She sighed. "You're right. This is an old folk's home. People pass away from natural causes all the time. I just hope

Reggie will listen to us when we tell him that his friend wasn't murdered."

Despite their best efforts, however, the old man refused to listen.

"I know what I heard. Beatrice was struggling with someone—she was being attacked. I thought you of all people would believe me." The look he gave Moira made her flinch. No one had ever looked at her with such disappointment in their eyes. Had she really let him down so much? Would Reggie ever forgive her?

# CHAPTER FIVE

The next few days passed in a blur of activity; despite her plans for taking it easy her first week home, both the deli and her personal life demanded her attention. It was easy to get back into the swing of things, but she occasionally found herself longing for a return to the tropical beaches and impeccable service of the cruise. The coffee that she brewed at home just could not compare to the exotic flavors that had gushed from the ship's espresso machines every morning. One thing that she did appreciate about being home was the privacy. On the cruise ship, the only time she was really alone was in her small room under the main deck; it was a wonderful feeling to be able to sit outside on the back porch and enjoy the peaceful morning without another soul within sight.

It wasn't until the weekend that she finally had a day off. Saturdays were one of their busiest days, but she had absolute faith that her employees would be able to handle anything routine that got thrown at them. She was looking forward to a well-deserved break from the deli, and the chance to catch up with her friends. She had met Denise and Martha on Wednesday morning for their weekly cup of coffee together, but none of them had been able to stay for long. She had barely finished telling them about everything that had happened on the cruise when she had picked up a call from Dante saying that the oven wasn't working. So she'd been forced to rush back to the deli before she got a chance to ask her two friends if they had done anything interesting since she had last seen them.

Taking advantage of the fact that she didn't have to wake up early to rush in to work, Moira slept in late on Saturday morning. She felt refreshed when she rose, and once again wondered what on earth she had been thinking when she changed the deli's hours to include breakfast. *Back when we opened in time for lunch, I was never out of bed before eight,* she thought. *Now I'm regularly up to my arms in food prep by seven.* She didn't regret the decision, though, not really. The deli was bringing in a lot more customers now, and the extra hours let her hire more employees. She was glad to be able to give the wonderful young people working for her a good job. One problem with living in such a small town was that employment was hard to come by outside of tourist season.

"I may not like waking up at dawn," she said out loud, talking to her dogs as she often did, "but I do love everything else about my job. And I still get to sleep in a couple of days every week. That's not too bad, is it?"

Maverick thumped his tail, not understanding her words, but nonetheless happy to hear her voice. Keeva came over from the other side of the bed to see what all the commotion was about, and shoved her cold, wet nose right into Moira's face. Wincing, the deli owner took this as a sign that it was time to start the day.

She had only a few hours of free time before she had to leave to go to a late lunch Karissa, David's sister, was hosting. Martha and Denise had also been invited. She was just itching to cook something to bring along, but the other woman had specifically told her that she didn't have to bring anything. Since her relationship with Karissa had had a bumpy start, she decided not to push it—she would accede to the woman's request and come empty-handed.

She spent the morning by taking a nice, long walk in the woods with the dogs while sipping from a travel mug of coffee. Her thoughts were on Reggie—she hadn't heard from him all week, and Candice had called a couple of days ago to tell her that the elderly man seemed depressed. Even though she knew she hadn't done anything intentionally wrong, Moira couldn't help feeling a sickening guilt at the thought of how betrayed Reggie must feel.

*He came to me for help, and I told him I didn't believe him,* she thought as she walked along the trail. The two dogs were gallivanting ahead of her, crisscrossing the path with their noses to the ground. She smiled, their obvious joy lifting her spirits. *I guess there's nothing else I could have done, short of lie to him. And even then I wouldn't have had the time to go chasing after a killer that didn't exist.*

"Come on, you two," she called as they rounded the last bend before the trail opened up to her yard. "It's time to go in."

Back inside she got the dogs settled, refilling their water bowl and checking them over for ticks, before heading upstairs to shower and get ready for the lunch with Karissa, Martha, and Denise. She was glad the three women had become friends. David's sister was new to town, and could certainly use people to talk to, and it never hurt to have someone else to bounce ideas off of. The only problem was that she still didn't feel quite as comfortable around Karissa as she felt around the others. How could she, considering the embarrassing mistake she had made of thinking Karissa was David's secret girlfriend when she first met her?

"I'm so glad you could make it," Karissa said as she opened her door to Moira's knock. "The others should be here soon. Lunch is almost ready… get back, Hazel. Let her get inside before sniffing her, at least."

The last part was directed toward the beautiful chocolate lab that had shoved her head between her mistress's leg and the door-frame. Not just her tail but her entire body was wiggling back and forth as she tried to get to Moira. The deli owner smiled, and after stepping inside and closing the door behind her, she crouched down and gave the excited dog some love.

"How's she settling in?" she asked Karissa.

"It's like she's been here her whole life."

A few weeks ago, a very pregnant Hazel had been abandoned behind Darling's DELIcious Delights. The deli owner had taken her in, unwilling to drop such a friendly dog off at the animal shelter— that was no place for puppies—and had ended up raising the entire litter until they were old enough to go to new homes. Karissa had originally planned on adopting one of the puppies, but had fallen in love with Hazel when they met and had ended up taking her home instead. Sending all the puppies and Hazel off to new homes had been an emotional experience for Moira, but she was confident that all of the dogs would be loved by their new owners.

Hazel certainly seemed happy with her new lot in life, and the deli owner didn't blame her. A plush dog bed lay by the couch, and there was a big basket of toys by the gas fireplace. The dog was wearing a nice new collar, with a brass nameplate riveted to the black leather.

"David got that for her," Karissa said as Moira admired the collar.

"It's nice," the deli owner said. "It looks great on her. She's a lucky dog."

Martha and Denise arrived within minutes of each other. By the time both women were inside and had found somewhere to set their purses and shoes, the oven timer was beeping. Karissa disappeared into the kitchen to check on the status of whatever it was she had made. Judging by the smell, whatever the dish was, it would taste amazing. Moira's stomach growled, and she exchanged a grin with Martha.

"Sorry I had to run out so quickly during coffee on Wednesday," she said. "Somehow the stove got unplugged, probably while one of us was cleaning, and it wasn't working. Would you believe it took Dante, Meg, and me half an hour before we finally thought to check the outlet?"

"At least it wasn't anything you needed a repairman for," the other woman said. Moira agreed. She had been terrified that one of the gas pipes had burst somewhere and that the entire deli would go up in flames at any minute.

"All right, it's time to eat," Karissa said, reappearing from the kitchen and carrying a casserole dish between two oven mitts. "Let me just set this down, and I'll bring the salad out."

The deli owner could tell even before serving herself the first spoonful of casserole that the meal was going to be delicious. Lightly browned breadcrumbs topped the dish, forming a crispy top over the creamy chicken, broccoli, carrots, peas, and rice that made up the rest of the casserole. The salad was crisp iceberg lettuce topped with cottage cheese, walnuts, and halved canned pears.

"This is amazing," Moira said after taking her first bite. It was the perfect meal to assuage her hunger, both filling and healthy.

"Thanks," the other woman replied, blushing. "I've been wanting to start cooking more since I moved here, though it's a hard resolution to stick to with two great restaurants nearby."

"Nothing beats homemade food," Denise said. "It may be easier to go out and pick up food from some place, but I've never found it as satisfying as eating something you make yourself."

The deli owner nodded. "That's one reason I love the deli so much. I love watching people enjoy the food that I make. It's a great feeling."

"It definitely is," Denise agreed. She owned the Redwood Grill, a nice steakhouse on the outskirts of Maple Creek. "Though I don't spend as much time in the kitchen these days. With two chefs, things are already pretty crowded."

Martha, who had been sitting quietly, listening to their conversation, chuckled. "At least you *can* cook. I'm lucky if I don't burn my oatmeal. I've done that before, in fact, and had to stop at the deli on the way to work and get one of Darrin's quiches. It was delicious and got me hooked—now I stop in at least twice a week for breakfast."

"You might want to stop in more often, now that we have the breakfast cookies," Moira said.

Martha groaned. "I love being your friend, but you and Denise are absolutely terrible for my waistline."

"I think we all have that problem," Karissa said. "That's another reason I wanted to start cooking for myself—if I don't start paying more attention to what I eat, I'm going to have to replace all of my pants with the next size up."

They laughed and chatted about food for a few more minutes. Then, as Moira was reaching for a second serving of chicken casserole, Karissa cleared her throat.

"How are things going with David?" she asked.

The deli owner smiled. "Good," she said. "Really good, I think."

"That's good." Karissa gave what almost seemed like a relieved smile. "You seem like you're good for him, Moira. I hope things work out."

The conversation continued, moving into the realm of future vacation plans. Moira smiled and laughed along with the rest of them, but she couldn't help wondering what Karissa's non sequitur about David had been about. Had the private investigator asked his sister to do some digging? If so, did it mean that David thought she was having doubts about their relationship? *I* have *been busy lately,* she thought. *I hope he doesn't think I've been avoiding him. He's one of the most important people in my life... I hope he knows that.*

# CHAPTER SIX

The concern that David might feel that she wasn't fully invested in their relationship lately stuck with her, so later that evening she called him to see if he was interested in getting dinner at the Redwood Grill the next night. He agreed and sounded happy enough over the phone. Eager to make the evening special, on Sunday she went shopping for a new dress after her deli shift ended. She was just packing the bag with her new dress—dark green with a pattern of white roses along the hem—into her SUV when her phone rang.

It was Candice.

"Mom, can you come to dinner tonight with me and Eli at Misty Pines?" she asked.

Moira bit her lip. "I'd love to, sweetie, but I've got plans with David. We're going to the Grill for dinner."

"He can come too," her daughter pleaded. "Reggie's really down, and Eli thinks talking to you will cheer him up. I guess he has some new ideas about that lady that died there last week."

The deli owner closed her eyes and leaned her forehead against her car. She didn't want to change plans with David at the last minute, but she already felt bad for Reggie. She owed it to him to go and hear him out, didn't she?

"I'll call David and see if he's okay with it," she said at last. "I'll let you know either way once I get in touch with him."

The private investigator answered his phone on the second ring, and quickly agreed to the change in plans. He didn't *sound* like he was upset, but Moira wanted to make sure.

"This is really all right with you?" she asked.

"Yes. I like Reggie, and it's been a while since I've seen Candice and Eli. It will be a nice dinner. Well... the company will be nice, anyway."

Even though Misty Pines had a private chef to cook for the residents, the food was always bland and soft. Many of the residents had special dietary needs, and it made more sense to make something that everyone could eat, and let people add the seasonings themselves, than to make a separate dish for each person. No matter how much salt she added to the beef stew, however, it would never compare to a steak at the Grill.

"I'm sorry, David. I really am. We can still eat out somewhere else later this week, okay?"

"Of course. And don't worry about tonight, Moira. I really don't mind." His voice was warm, but she still couldn't help but feel bad for changing plans at the last minute once again.

Her new dress was too fancy to wear to a casual dinner at the assisted-living home, so she stashed it in her closet when she got home and pulled on a blouse and pair of black slacks instead. Her mind switched back and forth from thoughts of David to thoughts of Reggie the entire time she was getting ready. They were both good men, and she had let them both down. She was certain she could make it up to David—he would forgive just about anything for a good, home-cooked meal—but Reggie would be harder. If he was still going on about Beatrice's death being a murder, she didn't know what she would do. Maybe it would be easier to just pretend to believe him after all. A little white lie like that would be all right, wouldn't it?

Misty Pines was bustling that evening. The dining room was already nearly full by the time she and David got there, but luckily Candice and Eli had arrived first and had snatched up an empty table for them. Reggie was sitting with them already, and was talking animatedly. He looked a lot better than he had the last time Moira had seen him, and she smiled.

"Hey guys," Candice squealed when she saw them. "Thanks so much for coming."

The deli owner hadn't had a chance to see her daughter much since they returned, and she was surprised at how tan the young woman still was. Of course, Candice had spent a lot more time out in the sun than she had… and she was still pretty tan herself, come to think of it.

"Hey, Ms. D," Eli said. "Mr. Morris. It feels like it's been ages since I've seen you."

"Only a couple of weeks," Moira said, but it did seem like it had been a long time to her, too. "How are you doing?" she asked Reggie.

"Not too bad. These old bones are still walking, and that's always a good thing." She looked at him, trying to decide if he was mad at her or not. He was smiling, and seemed to be in a good mood. She felt relieved.

"It sure is," she said. "So, what's for dinner tonight?"

The main course turned out to be baked chicken breast, green beans, and applesauce. The staff member waiting on them that night winked as he put a bottle of barbecue sauce next to David.

"So, how's the ice cream shop doing?" the private investigator asked as he slathered his chicken in sauce.

"Not bad for this time of year," Eli answered. "We'll close up for the season in a couple of months. Then I'll probably start spending more time helping Candice and Logan out at the candy shop."

Logan was Denise's nephew, a seventeen-year-old kid that Moira had hired to watch her dogs during her long days at work. When her daughter had announced that she was ready to hire her first employee, the deli owner had recommended him immediately. He was a good worker, and was okay with the small amount of hours that he got at the candy shop.

"We're doing really well," Candice added. "Logan took care of things while we were away, and I just put in another order for custom molds. Selling chocolates online was a great idea."

The young woman had a friend with a 3D printer that made her custom silicone molds at a good price. She had begun selling the custom-shaped candies online for weddings, parties, and even businesses that wanted a good way to spread their name.

"Remind me to order some from you," Moira said. "I've no doubt that my customers at the deli would love them, and it never hurts to have even more ways of advertising."

"Too bad it's not so easy to sell ice cream online," Eli said. "I'd be in business year-round."

The deli owner smiled. So far things were going well, and Reggie didn't seem upset at all. In fact, he hadn't mentioned Beatrice's death once, which was unusual for him. Eli's grandfather was one of the stubbornest people she knew. The reason for his good mood became obvious just a few minutes later, when a middle-aged man approached their table hesitantly.

"Um, sorry I'm late. Do you still want me to join you?" This was directed at Reggie, who nodded and gestured at the empty chair across from Moira.

"Make yourself comfortable, Danny."

The man, who had floppy mouse-colored hair and bloodshot grey eyes, sat down. He pulled the chair closer to the table, wincing as is scraped across the floor with a honking noise.

"I'm Danny Hatchfield," he said once he was settled. "Beatrice's son."

"Oh." Moira exchanged a glance with David. "Hello. It's nice to meet you."

"You, too. Reggie has been telling me so much about you. He was a close friend of my mother, and has really been helping me get through all of this."

"I'm so sorry about her passing," the deli owner said. "She must have meant the world to you."

"I hate to say it, but we actually weren't that close for a long time. I was just beginning to come around when... when she died. I feel horrible about it. I spent more time visiting my aunt—her sister—than I did visiting her."

"Is your aunt here, too?" she asked.

"Oh, yes. They were very close, and demanded to be put into the same home together. Other than me, they were the only family that they had."

"No one else?" Moira wondered aloud.

"No... my dad was in the military and never came back from his last deployment, and my aunt never got married. I'm an only child, so I had to do everything. Luckily, this place isn't too far away from where I work, and it's one of the nicer homes in the state."

"Well, even though you and your mother weren't close, you did step up and take care of her. I'm sure she knew that, and appreciated it."

"Thanks." He sighed. "This whole thing has been a nightmare. Her funeral is Tuesday, and if I'm being honest, I can't wait until it's over. Once her ashes are spread I'll finally be able to have closure."

The rest of the dinner was eaten in awkward silence. None of them were comfortable talking about personal matters with Danny there, and he didn't seem to have much else to say. Reggie looked triumphant, and kept shooting Moira meaningful glances. She avoided his gaze, not wanting to let him know what she was thinking until she got a chance to talk to David. Maybe someone having a motive to kill her wasn't enough reason to believe that Beatrice had been murdered, but surely her son was acting suspicious. He seemed more annoyed by her death than anything. *He says he can't wait until the funeral is over*, she thought. *She's getting cremated, so in just a couple of days there won't be a chance of anyone doing a full autopsy on her body. Isn't that just a little bit too convenient?*

She waited until she and David were driving home before telling him her concerns. He listened, but seemed reluctant to agree with her.

"I agree that Danny didn't seem too beat up about her death," he said. "But there are plenty of people who wouldn't be too sad to see their parents go. Not everyone has the same sort of relationship with their children that you do with Candice."

"She's getting cremated, though," Moira said. "And he said he can't wait until her funeral is over. Don't you think that's suspicious? He's probably getting her cremated her so no one will be able to dig up her body if people have suspicions later."

"Or she *wanted* to be cremated. It's a lot less expensive than a burial, and if she knew her son was having money problems—"

"That's another point," she interrupted. "From what Reggie said, Danny doesn't have much money at all. You saw his clothes today; they weren't the nicest. And he wasn't close to his mother—do you really think he would spend thousands every month to keep her in there, even if he *could* afford it? No, she must have had money of her own, and a lot of it. If he's the only living relative, then he's probably set to inherit it all. And since Danny was her immediate family member, he would have had the code to unlock the doors. It all makes perfect sense."

"This is all just conjecture," David said. He sighed, then added, "But you do have a point. I'm still not convinced, but I'll look into it for you if you want. I can do a background check on him, see what his financial situation is like, and if he has any priors."

"So does this mean I can tell Reggie we're investigating?"

"You can tell Reggie *I'm* investigating. Your only job is to keep in contact with him and tell me if he comes up with anything else, all right?"

Moira ground her teeth, but conceded. She hated it when David tried to keep her from investigating this sort of thing with him, but it wasn't like she really *wanted* something else on her plate right now. Between the deli, catering, and catching up on housework, she was already busier than she wanted to be. Besides, David knew what he was doing and had better resources than she did. She would just get in the way if she tried to investigate this on her own.

"Fine," she said. "You'd better tell Reggie not to go poking around either. I've got the feeling that he *wants* this to be a murder, and knowing him, he'll probably get into trouble trying to prove that he's right."

"I'll give him a call tomorrow," David said with a smile. He reached one arm over and draped it over her shoulder. "If only my paying clients needed my help as often as the two of you do, I'd be rich."

# CHAPTER SEVEN

By the time they got back to her house and David had kissed her goodbye, it was too late to call Reggie. Since she had to be up bright and early for the morning shift at the deli the next morning, she decided to call him them. She was certain he would be glad to hear that David was going to look into Danny's finances, and she was going to have to apologize for not taking him more seriously right away. There still wasn't any solid evidence that Beatrice had been killed, but her son certainly did seem like a suspicious character.

Up at the crack of dawn, Moira spent a significant amount of time grumbling about how much she hated early mornings while she waited for her coffee machine to gurgle out the last drops of her morning drink. By the time she had finished her first cup, she felt more like a normal human being and was even able to take a moment to appreciate just how beautiful the forest around her house was at sunrise. Sunlight filtered down from the canopy above, and the grass in her yard sparkled with dew. She opened the kitchen widow to let the birdsong in, then grabbed her cellphone to call Reggie.

Just as she had guessed, he was happy to hear her news. She had to admire his determination; he had manipulated her, David, and Danny into having dinner together so they could see just how suspiciously Danny was acting. Reggie might be old, but his brain was still sharp… most of the time.

By the time she got to the deli, all vestiges of sleepiness were gone and she found herself to be in an unusually good mood. An idea for a new flavor of breakfast cookie percolated in her mind, and she was eager to try it. Even better, Allison had called and asked if she could pick up some extra shifts to help pay for the online classes she was taking; so Moira suddenly had Wednesday completely off. She was already planning to make a big lunch, though she wasn't sure who she would invite—maybe Candice, and she could take the opportunity to catch her daughter up on Reggie's theory of Beatrice's murder.

Since Dante wouldn't be in for another half an hour, the deli was empty and still locked up when she got there. Humming to herself, she unlocked the front doors and slipped inside, pausing to turn the bolt behind her. She had had enough close calls that she no longer felt comfortable leaving the deli unlocked while she was there alone, but she still loved the feeling of being by herself in the building. With its fully stocked fridges and pantries, its state-of-the-art appliances, and the long, clean counters in the kitchen, the possibilities felt endless. She could make just about anything she wanted, and it was the best feeling in the world.

She began by preheating the oven, listening with satisfaction as the gas inside ignited. She grabbed one of the clean cookie sheets from the dish rack above the industrial sized sink and applied a non-stick coconut oil spray. Having skipped breakfast at her house, her mouth was already watering at the thought of the delicious cookies that she was about to make. *I'll only have one*, she promised herself, knowing that she would probably have a few of Dante's mini-quiches too. *I really need to come up with some low-calorie options. I'm sure my customers would appreciate it… and I know my scale would.*

She got to work, pulling a large glass mixing bowl out of the cupboard and dumping a few cups of steel-cut oats into it. She added a big dollop of almond butter, a couple of tablespoons of brown sugar, some crushed pecans, and then the most important ingredient—two cups of pure maple syrup.

After mixing it all together, she spooned clumps of the thick dough onto the cookie sheet and slid it into the oven while she wiped down the counters. Dante arrived just as the oven beeped, and she made him sit down to try them with her. She was so hungry that she burned her mouth on the first bite, but even through the pain she could tell that this was another delicious flavor.

"Good job, Ms. D," Dante said with appreciation. "I think I'll make the maple bacon quiches today—they should go along with the breakfast cookies perfectly."

"Set a couple aside for me, will you?" she asked. "I've got to put the last batch of cookies in, then I'm going to go start opening. We've been getting more business than ever for breakfast. People seem to really like these cookies."

"Everyone loves them," he said. "David bought half a dozen the other day. He said he was going to save them for lunch, but I'm pretty sure none of them even made it back to the office with him."

"When did David stop in?" she asked, surprised. He frequently stopped in at the deli, but always while she was there, and this week he had been too busy even for that.

"Oh, the other morning. I don't remember what day it was, but it was one of the days that you had the evening shift." He changed the subject with a somewhat flustered look on his face. "Anyway, Demi Goodwell said she wants some of the peanut butter banana ones for dessert when we cater her daughter's sweet sixteen party. I haven't marked it on the order form yet... I should probably go do that now."

Moira watched suspiciously as the young man hurried awkwardly out of the kitchen to grab the order form from under the register. Was he acting oddly, or was it all in her head? Frowning, she turned to check the time. It was later than she thought, and all thoughts of Dante were wiped out of her mind as she hurried to get the second batch of cookies in the oven before hungry customers started arriving.

She didn't think of Dante's awkward behavior again until Allison arrived shortly before the morning shift ended. The girl took one look at Moira and broke out in giggles.

"What?" she asked. "Do I have something on my face?" She had just guiltily eaten her third breakfast cookie—they had leftovers, what was she supposed to do… let them go to waste?—and was feeling self-conscious about it.

Allison shook her head, still grinning. "No, you look great, Ms. D." The young woman exchanged a glance with Dante and her grin widened. Moira stared after her, flabbergasted, until she disappeared through the kitchen door to drop her purse off and pick up her name tag.

"What's gotten into you two?" she asked Dante. Before he could say anything, she put her hand up, signaling him to wait. Someone was walking by on the sidewalk outside the deli, a woman that she recognized as the director of Misty Pines. If she wanted to do any digging on Beatrice's death on her own, this was her chance.

"Excuse me," she said, hurrying outside. "Um, Mrs. Radisson?"

"Huh? Oh, Moira. Do call me Alberta, dear." The woman turned to face her, smiling. "What can I do for you? I just dropped my car off at EZ Wheels down the road, so I've got some time to kill."

"Well in that case, come on in and have a breakfast cookie and a cup of coffee on me," the deli owner said. She lowered her voice, adding, "There's something I wanted to talk to you about... about Beatrice."

The other woman nodded, her expression serious. "Ah, Reggie's gotten to you, has he? Well, I'm happy to come in and take you up on that offer."

Alberta followed her inside, nodding as she looked around at the deli. She perched on a seat at a bistro table in the corner, and thanked Moira when she brought out a tray with two coffees and some of the maple pecan breakfast cookies on it.

"But don't you want one too?" she asked as she picked up a cookie.

The deli owner gave her a sheepish grin. "I've been eating them all morning," she admitted.

"They must be good," the other woman said with a chuckle. "I've been meaning to thank you personally for catering that event at Misty Pines a couple of months ago. The food was absolutely delicious. If you ever want a different job, I'd be happy to send our current chef packing."

"While it's tempting, my heart's with the deli," Moira said, smiling. "Thank you, though. I love hearing compliments like that."

"What was it you wanted to talk about?" the other woman asked. She took a bite of the breakfast cookie and added, "This is really good, by the way."

"It's a new flavor. I'm glad you like it." The deli owner took a sip of her own coffee, trying to decide how to broach the subject of Reggie and Beatrice. She decided to start with the phone call that she had gotten from the elderly man in the middle of the night, and go from there.

"I'm not sure what I think about all of this," she finished. "I didn't think there was anything to it at first, but after speaking to Danny… well, he doesn't seem a model son, exactly."

Alberta, who was on her second cookie, nodded. "He definitely wasn't. He had a very strained relationship with his mother— something about money, I think. He had a better relationship with his aunt, but I have the suspicion that she regularly loaned him large amounts of cash."

"Wow," the deli owner said, shaking her head. "He sounds like a real winner. Do you think he actually could have done it?"

"It's a possibility," the director said. "Thank you for telling me all of this. I knew about Reggie's concerns, but I didn't know the full story. I'll do what I can to reopen the investigation into Beatrice's death, but it might be hard since Danny has her power of attorney; without any evidence, I might have a hard time getting him to sign the morgue release. If he did kill her for her money, he's in for a nasty surprise, though. Beatrice made a new will shortly before she passed, and I can tell you that her son wasn't in it."

# CHAPTER EIGHT

For the next few days, Moira mulled over what Alberta had told her. The more she thought about it, the more likely it seemed that Beatrice's death wasn't from natural causes after all. What if Danny had heard that his mother had removed him from the will? He might have been so angry that he had decided to end her life then and there. It was a chilling thought, but it made a horrible sort of sense.

David, when she told him, didn't say much. Danny had never been in trouble with the law, as far as his background check said, anyway. He had one eviction under his belt, and had had credit collectors sent after him twice.

"I'm still not convinced," her told Moira over the phone Tuesday evening. "I know he *looks* guilty, but the fact is, her death was determined to be from natural causes. Wasn't her funeral today? She's probably long since been cremated, as I highly doubt that Danny would have made it easy for any sort of autopsy to be done. The police aren't going to listen to you without some sort of real evidence—can you imagine the chaos if they arrested someone whenever a rich old person with a bad relationship with their children died? They would never be able to get anything done at Misty Pines, because it would always be crawling with police."

"Well, how do I get evidence?" the deli owner asked, annoyed. "They've already cleaned out her room and given it to someone else, and I doubt Danny will let me search his house for a possible murder weapon. I don't want him to just get away with this, David. If he killed her, he deserves to spend a very long time in jail. The woman raised him, for goodness sake."

"I guess I could do some digging and see if I can find out who Beatrice put in her will if it wasn't him," he said. "They might be able to at least shed more light on Danny's relationship with his mother."

"All right… thanks, David. I know this is taking up a lot of your time, and I appreciate it. Are you sure you can't make lunch tomorrow? Candice and Eli are both coming."

"Sorry, but I'm going to be in Traverse City. One of my clients thinks her husband is cheating on her, and he's leaving for a 'business trip' tonight. I've got to keep an eye on him."

"Oh, let me know what happens. I hope he's innocent."

"I don't," David said, surprising her.

"What?"

"His wife's going to divorce him either way, she just thinks it will look better for her if he's an adulterer. For his sake, it will be better if he's not the loving husband that he appears to be. Otherwise, he's going to be crushed."

"She sounds like a terrible woman," Moira said. "You work with the strangest people."

"I know." She could hear the smile in his voice. "It's how I met you, remember?"

Even though David wouldn't be coming to her lunch on Wednesday, it didn't stop her from going all out. It had been a while since she had cooked a big, multi-course meal, and she was looking forward to it. In the morning, she went shopping, buying mostly fresh ingredients, and also picking up a couple of soup bones for the dogs. At home she tossed the marrow-filled bones out onto the back porch and let the dogs outside, knowing that they would be kept happily busy for the next few hours.

Her kitchen was a lot smaller than the deli's kitchen, but still had everything that she needed to make a three-course meal. She began with the fish: thick swordfish steaks that she seasoned with garlic and lemon pepper. After covering the glass dish with plastic wrap, she set the fish in the fridge to keep it fresh until she was ready to put it in the oven. The next part of the meal was creamy cauliflower soup, and she chopped up the white florets and put them in a pot of boiling water while she turned her attention to the salad.

In no time at all, a big bowl of fresh greens and veggies was sitting on the table, along with a few different varieties of dressing. The fish was cooking in the oven, and the cauliflower soup was simmering away on the stove. To complete the meal, Moira got out a chilled bottle of chardonnay out of the fridge and set it on the table. She had gone all out with the place settings, even digging up a tablecloth. *It looks good*, she thought, wishing that David could be there to appreciate it.

"Wow, Mom, it smells amazing in here," said Candice when she and Eli arrived a few minutes later. "You didn't need to go to all of this trouble just for us."

"I wanted to," Moira replied with a smile. "You're my daughter… and I've come to realize just how special it is that we have such a good relationship."

She was thinking of Danny and his mother Beatrice again. How on earth could someone kill their own parent? It was a horrible thought, and it made her glad that she and her daughter got along so well.

"I just wish David could have come," she added as they sat down. "We haven't had much of a chance to see each other lately."

Candice bit her lip and looked over at Eli before replying. "I'm sure it's only temporary," she said. "You've been so busy getting back into the swing of things after the cruise, and he's been completely slammed at work. Things will calm down eventually."

"Did he tell you he was busy at work?" Moira asked, frowning. Why did it seem that David had time to talk to everyone but her?

"Yeah, he stopped in at the candy store the other day to chat, only for a few minutes," her daughter said. "But Mom, let's eat. This fish looks delicious. What is it?"

The conversation steered away from personal matters as Moira and Candice began reminiscing about their time together on the cruise. Eli took second helpings of the cauliflower soup and listened while the women talked.

"I've got to ask," he said at last. "Didn't you ever get bored, spending all of your time on a boat? I mean yeah, it's a big boat, but I feel like I'd go stir-crazy."

"Well we got to stop at some islands," Moira said. "And there was a *lot* to do on the cruise. I think the hardest part for me was being around so many people for so long. It made me appreciate this quiet country house even more."

"I loved it," Candice said. "Everyone was super nice and happy, and there was always something to do."

It wasn't until Moira brought out dessert—homemade brownies with caramel drizzled on top—that she broached the subject of Reggie. She gathered that he had mentioned his concerns to Eli and Candice, but not in as much detail.

"No wonder he wanted you to come to dinner Sunday evening so badly," Eli said. "I'd wondered. He was very adamant that you were there. He mentioned it being something about Beatrice, but I didn't pay much attention. I'm sorry to say it, but I thought he was imagining things."

"So did I at first," Moira admitted. "David still isn't completely convinced, but I think Reggie's on to something."

"He may be," Eli said. "I'll do some digging, too. I'm at Misty Pines all the time, so it will be easy for me to ask around. Maybe one of Beatrice's friends knows why she changed her will."

"See if you can talk to her sister," the deli owner said. "According to Danny, they were close. If anyone knows anything, she does."

# CHAPTER NINE

The next morning, Moira got a call from Eli. He was excited, and she had to put down her coffee and ask him to go over it again.

"It's about Beatrice's sister," he said. "Her name's Delilah. She's even older than Beatrice was, but she seems to know what's going on... and guess what?"

"What?"

"She says she knows her sister was killed, and she has a good idea about who did it. I guess someone's been bugging her about her own will, but she had to go and do her morning exercises before she could tell me who. She wants to meet us for lunch and talk about it—oh, and she wants you to bring a fast food burger. She said she's sick of the food here and wants something unhealthy for once. Will you be able to come?"

"Lunch today?" Moira glanced at her watch. She had to be at the deli by one to relieve Meg. "I can come for a cup of coffee at noon, but I can't stay for long. I'll bring her burger as long as it won't get me in trouble with the nurses."

"Perfect," Eli said. "I can't believe Grandpa was actually right. He's always concocting mysteries where they don't exist, but this is twice now that he's actually been onto something. Bring David if you can. See you soon, Ms. D!"

She and David pulled up to the retirement home shortly before noon. She clutched a small fast food bag, and kept glancing nervously at her phone; she had called Eli a few minutes ago to tell him they were nearly there, but he hadn't answered.

"I hope she hasn't changed her mind about talking to us," she said to David as they walked through the first set of heavy doors. "If she really knows who killed her sister, she might be in danger if she tells us."

They had to buzz twice before anyone came to unlock the second set of doors.

"I'm sorry," the harried-looking nurse said as she let them in. "One of our residents just passed away, so we're all busy. It's fine for you to come in as long as you stay out of the way when the paramedics arrive."

Moira's stomach swooped.

"Who was it?" she asked.

"Delilah Ford," the nurse said. "Did you know her?" She must have seen the shocked expression on Moira's face.

"No," the deli owner said faintly. "Not really."

The nurse walked away, leaving them to find an out-of-the-way spot to stand. The assisted-living home was busy, with staff rushing back and forth, and most of the residents ignored them. She was just opening her mouth to wonder aloud to David if this could possibly be a coincidence when Eli rounded the corner and waved them over. His expression was grim.

"We're meeting in my grandfather's room," he said. "I take it you heard?"

She nodded as they followed him. On their way, they passed a man even older than Reggie, sobbing quietly into a handkerchief.

"That's Griff," Eli said softly. "I guess he was close to Delilah. They spent most of their time together."

*How sad*, she thought. *To lose someone so close to him so suddenly...*

When they got to Reggie's room, Moira was surprised to see her daughter there too, pacing back and forth in front of the window. The old man sat in an armchair, a frown creasing his brow.

"Delilah knew," he said once Eli had closed the door behind her and David. "She knew, and she got killed for it."

"Did she tell you who the killer was?" Moira asked him. He shook his head.

"She got rushed away for morning exercises before she could. I didn't know her very well, not like I knew Bea. She didn't even know that I suspected murder until Eli here tracked her down and asked her about her sister's death."

"How did she die?" the private investigator asked.

"I heard one of the nurses say she passed peacefully in her sleep during a nap," said Eli. "But I don't know much more than that. We got shooed away as soon as they caught us listening."

"I feel terrible," Moira said, setting down the bag containing the hamburger that Delilah would never get a chance to eat. "There's no way this is a coincidence. I just don't believe that two sisters passed peacefully in their sleep weeks apart from each other. Add in the accusations of murder, and it's even more suspicious."

"Reggie," Candice said suddenly. "You have to stop telling people that you think Beatrice was killed. If whoever did it is trying to cover their tracks, then you might be in trouble too."

"I'm not keeping quiet about this, young lady," Reginald said firmly. "I can't just turn my head and ignore the fact that two women—one of them a close friend—have been murdered inside these walls."

"I know it's hard," David said. "But she's right. We don't want to see you get hurt, Reggie."

"Who else is going to find the killer?" he grumbled. "None of you believes me."

"We do now," Moira said with a glance at the private investigator. "And we should have before. I'm sorry that we didn't. Just be careful, please? We'll keep poking around, but it might be dangerous for you to do so."

He nodded reluctantly. She wondered if they could trust him to keep to himself, but knew they didn't really have a choice. *If only I had believed him in the first place, this may not have happened,* she thought guiltily. *I could have gone to the police right away, and somehow have convinced them to do a full autopsy on Beatrice. They might have found something in time to save her sister, and could have caught the killer without putting Reggie in danger like this.*

"I really am sorry," she told him in a softer voice. "I should have trusted you, Reggie. I'll do my best to make up for it."

"What do we do now?" Eli wondered. "Call the police and have them bring Danny in?"

"There still isn't any evidence that he's guilty," David pointed out.

"They might find something when they do an autopsy," Candice said.

"Will they even do an autopsy?" the deli owner asked. "Don't they only do that if they suspect something suspicious about the death?"

"There's a few reasons why they would want to do an autopsy, but it's likely that this death wouldn't need one," the private investigator said. "She was elderly, and if she had any sort of dangerous medical condition, her physician will probably just sign off on her death... as long as there were no signs of a struggle, of course. They might do an autopsy if a family member requested it, but if Danny is really her only living family member... well, that isn't likely."

"Do you think he killed his aunt, too?" she asked. "He did say he liked her."

"And Mrs. Radisson told you that she thought his aunt had given him a lot of money, didn't she? Maybe he didn't actually like her, he just hung around for the money."

"And if she knew that he killed his mother," Moira said, suddenly seeing the big picture, "Then she would have cut him off from the money and probably threatened to call the police on him."

They fell silent as they connected the dots. It was chilling to think that someone could have killed two of his family members just for money.

"What now?" Candice asked at last. "How can we get the police to believe us?"

"I don't know," David admitted. "If I can get them to see how suspicious the connection between the two deaths is, then they might be able to perform an autopsy even if Danny objects. I'll go and talk to Detective Jefferson after this. I want the rest of you to keep your heads down and your eyes open. Danny has already killed two people, let's not let him kill any more."

# CHAPTER TEN

Moira felt guilty for not believing Reggie at first. At least now she and David were both confident that he had been right about the murder, but it had taken a second death to convince them. How could she make it up to him? *Food*, she thought. *He must be just as sick of the nursing home food as all of the other residents are. I could have him over for dinner—I just need to get a list of what he can and can't have.*

The list was the easy part. All she had to do was phone Misty Pines, and one of the nurses emailed it to her. Figuring out what to make was harder. His diet wasn't as limited as some of the residents', but he couldn't have much sodium, fat, or anything hard to chew. She decided to fall back on what she was most comfortable making: soup.

She ended up making a delicious low-sodium cabbage and beef soup with a side of mashed potatoes and broccoli florets. Everything was on his list of safe foods, but it was all much more flavorful than the food normally was at the retirement home. Reggie, when she had called to invite him, had been thrilled; not just at the chance to eat normal food, but also to get out of the assisted-living home entirely.

"I know it's a nice place," he told her. "And I'm grateful to Eli for putting me here instead of a cheaper place, but when you get down to it, it's just a comfy jail."

Moira didn't tell him, but she secretly agreed. She knew that the locked doors were there to keep the residents safe, since some of them had psychological issues that made them a danger to themselves, but it still didn't seem right that none of the residents were allowed to leave unless they were checked out by a friend or family member. *By the time I need to go to a home, I probably won't care*, she told herself. *I'll probably enjoy the chance to put my feet up and relax while someone else does all of the cleaning, shopping, and cooking.*

Moira put the dogs in the mudroom behind a baby gate before Reggie got there. She knew they wouldn't purposely hurt him, but they were so big that they could easily push him over. He walked with the aid of a cane, and from what she had seen, he wasn't particularly steady on his feet.

Eli and Candice hadn't been able to make it, but David had volunteered to come, and was even driving Reggie from the nursing home to her house and back again. She had protested at first, not wanting him to go out of his way for something that was her idea, but he had insisted.

"You're making the whole dinner," he told her. "You don't need to be driving into town and back again too. I'll handle it. Besides, it will give me a chance to pick his brain. Maybe he'll be able to remember something else about Beatrice's or Delilah's deaths."

In the days between their meeting at Misty Pines and the dinner, Reggie had met with Detective Jefferson to discuss their suspicions about the two deaths. Amazingly, the detective had listened and agreed to see what he could do about ordering an autopsy on Delilah's body. It was a big step forward, and all three of them eagerly awaited news.

David and Reggie pulled up in the driveway shortly past five. Moira had the meal ready and waiting for them, and the table nicely set for Reggie's apology dinner. She was still mentally kicking herself for not believing him sooner, but at least he didn't seem upset with her.

"Thanks for coming," she said as she opened the front door for them.

"A chance to get out of that place and eat some good food for once?" he said. "I wouldn't have turned down this invitation even if Danny was the one that sent it."

"Don't say that," she said with a shudder. "If he knows that you're the reason the police are going to order an autopsy; you very well could be his next target."

"Oh, I'm going to be fine," he said with a casual wave of his hand. "Don't tell any of them at Misty Pines, but I had someone bring me one of those rubber door stops. No one is getting into my room if I don't want them to, even if they have a key."

"That, um, seems dangerous," she said, raising her eyes to meet David's. He shrugged, looking amused.

"How's it dangerous?" Reggie asked, seating himself in the chair that she pulled out for him. "I don't want a killer coming into my room again. There's nothing dangerous about that."

"But what if you fall or have a stroke, and the nurses can't get in in time to help you?" she asked.

"If it's my time, it's my time," he said nonchalantly. "Now, this smells delicious. Let's eat."

*I'm going to have to tell Eli about that doorstop*, she thought as she sat down across from him. David took the seat next to her and squeezed her hand before putting his napkin into his lap.

"This does look amazing, Moira," he told her. "Have you served this soup at the deli before?"

"A couple of times last year," she said. "I may bring it back again this winter."

"Mmm, restaurant-quality food." Reggie rubbed his hands together expectantly. "It's been too long."

"Well, dig in," she told him. "It's all healthy, so I don't think I'll get in trouble with any of your nurses. I've got dessert too, but you'll have to wait to find out what that is."

The dinner was a success. She doubted that it had been necessary to get Reggie to forgive her for not believing him—he seemed to have done that already—but it was nice to see him enjoy the meal so much. For a moment she was half-tempted to take up the director's offer of working as the chef at Misty Pines. It would be nice to have this much appreciation for her cooking every day. *It's not like my regular customers don't appreciate it*, she told herself. *They're just used to it.*

About halfway through the meal, David got a call on his cellphone. He glanced down at it, then stood up.

"Sorry," he said, "but I've got to take this."

A moment later he returned, sliding the phone back into his pocket. "I've got news."

"What?" said Moira and Reggie at almost exactly the same time.

"They got the autopsy report on Delilah back. Normally it takes longer, but they rushed it. Apparently Danny bought a one-way ticket to South America, and Detective Jefferson worried that he was getting ready to leave the country for good." David paused. "I'm not really supposed to be telling you this. Can you both keep it mum?"

"Of course," Moira said. Reggie nodded.

"According to the autopsy, Delilah suffocated. They think she was smothered by a pillow or a blanket—they found fibers in her lungs. Her death has officially been labeled a homicide."

"That's great," Reggie said enthusiastically. Then he cleared his throat and added, "I don't mean that she was killed, but that they're finally investigating it."

"I understand," Moira told him. "It *is* good. Hopefully they can arrest Danny soon, before he gets on that plane."

She felt relieved at the news. Her part in all of this was done. The police would handle it now, and if they moved quickly, then hopefully no one else would get killed.

"Dessert time," she announced, feeling like a weight had been taken off her shoulders. "I hope you both like apple crumble."

# CHAPTER ELEVEN

After they had each downed a couple of servings of warm apple crumble and low-fat ice cream, David left to drive Reggie back to Misty Pines. Moira started on the dishes, and was about halfway through when the private investigator returned.

"Dinner was nice," he said, coming up behind her and kissing her on the cheek before reaching into the sink to help her wash the remaining dishes. "I think it meant a lot to Reggie."

"Thanks for driving him," she said. "I still feel bad that you had to go out of your way. You don't even know him that well."

"I know him about as well as you do," he pointed out. "He seems like a good guy. He has interesting stories to tell—he's lived quite the life."

She had spent so much time doing everything alone that it felt odd, but nice, having a partner to hand bowls to for drying. *I want this all the time*, she thought as their arms brushed.

After the dining room table was cleared and the kitchen was cleaned up, they went out back with the dogs. The only seating Moira had on the back porch was a single rocking chair, so they leaned against the railing together instead of sitting as they watched the dogs play in the yard

"Do you think they'll arrest Danny before he flees?" she asked him.

"Honestly? I don't know." He paused, then added, "I'm less concerned with him being caught than him not hurting anyone else. I'd rather him escape with all of his aunt's money and live out the rest of his life on some beach in Argentina than have him get caught after attacking someone else."

She knew he was concerned about Reggie. The old man had been so vocal about the murders that he was the obvious next target if Danny was hanging around.

"If Danny knows that the police are investigating his mother's and aunt's deaths, then he might not take the chance of killing someone else," she said. "It would just give the police more to work with."

"I hope you're right." He ran his fingers through his hair and closed his eyes. "I wish he hadn't called you."

"Why?" she asked, surprised. "If it wasn't for him, then Delilah's death might never have been exposed as a murder."

"That's true," he said. "But I hate that you're involved. I wanted to keep you safe after you came back... but it looks like I failed miserably."

"I'm perfectly safe," she said. "No one has made any threats against me. I've hardly even talked to anyone from the nursing home. I don't think I even said anything to Danny that would make him think I suspect him to be the killer."

"Still, you're connected to Reggie." David shook his head. "I'm sorry, I just worry about you. I swear, I have twice the number of grey hairs now than before I met you."

"You don't need to worry so much," she said, reaching over and taking his hand. "I know a lot of crazy stuff has happened, but I'm fine."

"Moira, last month you almost died in a barn fire. You had a broken arm and passed out from smoke inhalation. Before that, you got a concussion and were almost shot. I honestly don't know whether you are the luckiest person that I've ever met, or the unluckiest."

"I think I'm the luckiest," she said. "If I was so unlucky, then I wouldn't have met you, would I ?"

He chuckled. "Well, it is hard to argue with that."

She smiled up at him, thinking back to all the times he had saved her. She really *was* lucky to have met him. Without him, chances were she wouldn't be standing there right then.

"I'm sorry we've both been so busy lately," he added. "We still haven't had a chance to go out for our nice dinner."

"How about Friday?" she said. "I work in the morning, and even though it's one of the busier nights, it's almost a week away. I'm sure Denise will be able to get us a table if I call her tomorrow."

"That sounds perfect." He squeezed her hand. "I can't wait."

They went inside a few minutes later, when the hungry mosquitoes became too much to bear. Moira checked the calendar and saw it was almost time for the dogs' next dose of heartworm medication; since her mind was on it, she popped open the package and gave them both their chewable beef-flavored pills.

"Oh, I saw the collar you got for Hazel," she told David. "I love it. It's so perfect for her."

"She's a sweet dog," he said. "Karissa loves her. It was nice of you to let her have Hazel."

"It was a weight off my back," she admitted. "Everyone wants a puppy. Not too many people want an adult dog with an unknown history."

"Really?" He looked down at Keeva and Maverick, who were both laying on the cool kitchen floor, tired from their play outside. "You took a chance on two of them."

"Well, they both kind of chose me," she said. "I couldn't very well abandon them after that, now could I?"

The dogs, somehow sensing that they were the topic of the conversation, looked up at her and David and started wagging their tales. The private investigator crouched down to scratch their ears.

"Oh, I haven't heard any more mice," she said, remembering the last time David had been at her house.

"Huh?" he said distractedly. Keeva had rolled over, and he was rubbing her belly.

"Remember, last time you were here you said that Maverick heard mice in the attic?"

"I don't—oh, right, I remember." He stood up, brushing his hands off. "Funny, huh? They must have left. Or maybe it was just the wind."

"Yeah," she said. "I guess." David really was acting strange lately.

# CHAPTER TWELVE

The next day at the deli was unusually slow, which for once was a good thing. Moira took the time to update the deli's website while Darrin organized the fridge. They had a catering event early next week, and they had to make sure that they had enough space to store the extra food that would be coming in the next delivery.

Martha stopped in after she got off work, a little bit after five. Seeing her friend was a nice change of pace for the deli owner, who had spent the last few hours coming up with the daily specials for the next two weeks.

"Slow day?" she asked, looking around at the empty dining area.

"I blame the weather," Moira said. It was an unusually warm, clear day, and most of her customers were probably at the beach for a last swim before the water got too cold. She was sure that Candice would find her way over to Lake Michigan after the candy shop closed—she would have been tempted to go herself if she hadn't already scheduled herself to work until close.

"Ugh, I didn't even notice," Martha said, glancing out the window. "I've been absolutely slammed at work. Speaking of, do you think you could watch Diamond for me this weekend? I can drop her off before your date with David."

Diamond was Martha's little black-and-white mixed-breed dog. The little pup had a wonderfully happy personality, and loved to play with Moira's two bigger dogs. She was small, but she was agile enough to run circles around them.

"Sure… wait, how do you know about our date?"

"Denise told me," her friend said.

"Oh…" Moira frowned, wondering if she was losing her mind. She hadn't called to make the reservation yet, had she? *David must have done it*, she realized. *That was nice of him.*

"You know what, I can find someone else to watch her this weekend," her friend said.

"No, no, it's really no trouble."

"You might be too busy…"

"I don't have any plans that weekend, other than work," the deli owner said. "I love having Diamond over, and so do my dogs. It'll be fun."

"If you're sure," her friend said anxiously.

"I am," Moira said firmly. She had no idea why her friend was being so weird about it. She usually watched Diamond a couple of times a month, when Martha traveled for her job. It was easier than putting Diamond in a kennel every time her owner had to go away, and the little dog enjoyed staying with Moira and two giant companions much more than sleeping alone in a kennel.

"Well, thank you. I really appreciate it." The other woman smiled at her and changed the subject. "I'm starved. What's the special today?"

"Asiago beef soup and a cheese and beef rye sandwich."

"That sounds perfect. Can I have a cup of soup and a sandwich, and one of these carbonated waters?"

"Sure thing. Coming right up."

She poked her head into the kitchen to tell Darrin the order and ask him to bring out a second serving for her, then joined her friend at a table. They chatted about their jobs while they waited for the food, then fell silent as they both dug in. Moira was about halfway through her soup when she heard her phone, still in her purse behind the register, go off. Excusing herself, she got up and hurried over to catch it on the final ring.

"I've got news," David said.

"Is it about Danny?" she asked. "Did the police arrest him."

"Yes, and no. I got in touch with Beatrice and Delilah's lawyer—it turns out that they used the same one—and told him I was investigating their deaths. I told him my theory about Danny being the killer, and that I thought he might have killed his mother when he found out that she took his name off of her will. He told me who she put in his place... it was Delilah."

"She left everything to her sister?" Moira asked, talking quietly so Martha wouldn't be able to hear what she was saying.

"Everything," David confirmed. "Not a single cent to Danny."

"Well, that might have been what made him angry enough to kill her," she said. "And he probably would have been upset with Beatrice as well. Wait... who did Beatrice put in *her* will?"

"That's the interesting part," he said. "The lawyer told me that Delilah made a change to her own will around the same time that Beatrice did."

"Well, who did she put down?"

"I don't know," the private investigator said. She could hear his frustration through the phone, and could almost see the muscles in his jaw flexing as he fought not to grind his teeth—an old habit that he had been trying to break since a recent trip to the dentist. "The lawyer started getting suspicious, wondering exactly how much he had to tell me. He wasn't too happy to learn that he didn't technically have to tell me *anything*. A private investigator's badge doesn't mean people have to talk to you. Once he realized that, he clammed up."

"Well, at least you managed to get something out of him," she said. "I just wish we knew whether or not Danny stands to inherit anything from his aunt. If he was the person she named in her will, then he's going to be getting a *lot* of money. He'll get everything from both his aunt and his mother."

"No wonder he bought a one-way ticket out of the country," David said. "The second he boards that plane Thursday evening, he'll be free to do whatever he wants with his inheritance."

"That just means we have to stop him before his flight," the deli owner replied with determination.

"I don't want you getting involved with this again, Moira," he said. "He's already killed two people. Will you please leave this to the professionals?"

She mumbled something that might have sounded like agreement, told him she loved him, and hung up. It wasn't that she wanted to find herself hip deep in trouble again, but if the opportunity arose to put a stop to Danny's killing spree, she had no doubt that she would take it.

# CHAPTER THIRTEEN

"Sorry, Maverick," she said to her dog the next evening as she pulled on her boots. "I can't bring you this time. I promised Candice I'd help her with a big order of chocolates, which means we're going to be spending a lot of time in the kitchen, and I doubt any of her customers want to find a dog hair in their candy."

The big black and tan dog continued looking at her hopefully, his eager eyes not doing anything to make her feel better about leaving him behind. Keeva, on the other hand, seemed to have gotten the message. She lay on the hallway floor with her head between her paws, looking up at Moira with a mournful expression that wasn't much better than Maverick's eager whining.

"My goodness, you two act like I'm abandoning you. I'll only be gone for a few hours, and I'll see if Candice has any of those peanut butter biscuits that you like so much left."

The young woman had begun making homemade dog treats after finding an easy recipe online. She kept a bowl of free samples next to the register for her dog-loving customers to take. The biscuits were a big hit with both Maverick and Keeva, and were probably a lot healthier for them than the store-bought kind that they usually ate.

"Be good," she said, waggling a stern finger at them before she left. "If neither of you get into the bathroom trash while I'm gone, then we'll go on a nice long walk after I get back, all right?"

When her daughter had called her that morning, frantic because Logan, her only employee, was down with the flu, Moira had been only too happy to offer her help. She didn't know the first thing about chocolate making, but she figured it couldn't be too hard to pour melted chocolate into the silicon molds and stick them in the freezer. It would give her a chance to spend some time with her daughter, and, even better, it would serve as a nice distraction from worrying about Danny.

The clock to his departure was ticking ever closer. Neither she nor David had heard anything about the police department's investigation, and the silence was driving her crazy. In just two days, Danny would get on that plane and would be beyond the reach of their local police department. The worst part was the fact that there was nothing Moira could do about it, short of physically holding Danny back. David had already told the police everything that they knew. The station had even sent Officer Catto, one of their junior detectives, out to Misty Pines to talk with several residents, including Reggie and the staff; but according to Reggie they had barely mentioned Danny.

All in all, it was a stressful situation, and Moira was glad for an excuse to force herself to stop worrying about it. An evening spent in the kitchen with her daughter making chocolates sounded like just what she needed.

Candice's Candies was closed for the evening, the neon sign off, and a curtain drawn across the big front window. The deli owner drove by slowly, admiring the building from the front before continuing around the block to park in the back. She started toward the small door that led to the two apartments above the candy shop, then stopped herself. Candice had lived above the shop up until a few weeks ago, but now she lived across town in the big, old house of Reggie's that Eli lived in. The house was almost half again the size of her own stone house in Maple Creek, and had a private fenced-in yard, a sizeable deck in the back, and more bedrooms than they would ever need. Moira had been there a couple of times for dinner, and had to admit to herself that she was just the slightest bit jealous of her daughter's home, though she loved her little house in the woods.

She changed course and knocked instead on the back entrance of the candy shop, which was opened a split second later by an exhausted Candice.

"Thanks so much for coming, Mom," she said. "I know it's not Logan's fault—he was willing to come in despite being sick, but I couldn't chance it and told him to stay home—but it's been so hard trying to fulfill this order without him. Maybe I should begin thinking about hiring someone else... we've been getting a *lot* of online orders for our custom candies."

"We should hold some sort of job fair," Moira said, only half joking. "I've been thinking of hiring some new people just for the deli's catering service. It's hard splitting up the team I have now between catering and watching the deli."

Candice laughed and stood aside so her mother could go in. "You know, we really shouldn't be complaining. We have it pretty good when business is going *too* well."

"That's true. But one botched catering event—or delivery—would be terrible for our reputations. It's too easy to make a mistake when you've been working twelve-hour shifts all week."

"Ugh." The young woman scrunched her face up. "Don't remind me. I'm looking forward to some long days until Logan gets better. It will be nice when Eli closes shop for the season and can spend more time here. I think he's better at running this place than me and Logan are combined."

"He's had years more experience at running a business than you have," Moira pointed out. "Don't worry, you'll get there. The deli was a mess when I first opened it, but look at it now… things run pretty smoothly for the most part."

Making the chocolates turned out to be a simpler process than the deli owner had imagined. Candice obviously knew what she was doing, and smoothly moved from one double boiler to the next, giving the contents a stir and occasionally adding an extra dash or drop of this or that flavoring. Moira did her best to keep the counters clean, and hurried to help her daughter whenever she requested something.

"Can you take the molds out of the fridge and begin putting the chocolates in that box over there?" her daughter asked. "Put parchment paper between the layers, and when it's full, close the box and call me over so I can label it. Then the molds get washed and used again for the next batch."

The deli owner got to work, careful not to break any of the chocolates as she popped them out of the mold. They were in the shape of a paw print, with the letters CAHS stamped into them.

"What are these for?" she asked as she worked.

"Oh, it's the Capital Area Humane Society," the young woman replied. "They're having a fundraising event for the animals. The person I got Felix from gave them my name."

Felix was Candice's one-in-a-million male calico cat. Moira watched him once in a while when her daughter was away, and held a special spot of fondness for him in her heart.

"How is Felix doing? It's been a while since I've seen him. I bet he missed you while you were gone."

"Eli said he slept on my pillow every night," her daughter said, smiling as she sifted some confectioners' sugar into one of the double boilers. "He was definitely happy to see me again—he tried to climb up my leg when I walked in the door. I still have some scratches."

"It sounds like he still thinks he's a tiny kitten," Moira said, laughing. "I bet that was pretty unpleasant. His claws are like needles."

They worked in silence for a few more minutes, the deli owner focusing on laying the chocolates out in nice rows on each layer of parchment paper. She sensed her daughter glancing over at her periodically, and got the sense that there was something on her mind. When Candice spoke up at last, it was to ask something completely unexpected.

"Mom, do you love David?" she asked.

"Yes," Moira said, setting the box of chocolates aside so she could focus on her daughter. "I do."

"Like, as much as you loved Dad?"

She was surprised. Her daughter rarely brought up Mike these days. His death had hit Candice hard, despite there being both physical and emotional distance between them. Wondering what the young woman was getting at, she considered her answer carefully, trying to remember the days when she had first been married to her ex-husband.

"It's a different sort of love," she said at last. "Back when I met your father, I wasn't much older than you are now. I didn't really know what I wanted back then, or what kind of man I wanted to be with. I was infatuated with your father, but it just wasn't the kind of love that lasted… on either of our parts. What I feel for David is much deeper."

The young woman nodded. "Good."

Moira was about to ask her daughter why she wanted to know, wondering if she was having doubts about her relationship with Eli, when Candice's phone buzzed on the counter beside the stove. The young woman glanced over at it, then quickly wiped her hands on a hand towel and answered it.

"Hello?" she said. She was silent for a moment as she listened, and Moira saw her visibly pale. "We'll be right over."

"What's going on?" Moira asked once her daughter had hung up the phone.

"Someone else was just killed at the nursing home," Candice said. She frowned, as if still trying to make sense of it in her own mind. "It was Danny."

# CHAPTER FOURTEEN

At first Moira thought that Candice meant that Danny had killed someone else, but by the time they had turned off the stoves and done what they could to salvage the last of the chocolate, she realized that her daughter meant that Danny had been killed. Her mind was reeling. What did this mean? Had Danny been innocent all along, or had the murderer been avenging the deaths of Beatrice and Delilah? Had Reggie…? *No,* she told herself firmly as she yanked her seatbelt across her chest. *Don't even think it. Reggie wouldn't hurt anyone.*

As she put the SUV into gear, she asked Candice to give David a call and tell him what was going on. She was certain that he would want to be there, and he probably had a better chance than either of them at finding out what was going on.

"Is everyone else all right?" she asked her daughter once the call to the private investigator had ended.

"As far as I know," Candice said. "Eli was in the courtyard with his grandfather when it happened. He said he'd tell us more when we got there. A lot of people are pretty shaken up."

Misty Pines was only a few short minutes away from Candice's Candies, but the drive seemed to take an eternity. The parking lot was swarming with police and emergency vehicles when they got there, and they ended up parking in one of the farthest spots from the doors.

"Do you think they'll let us in?" Moira said, suddenly concerned that they would be barred from the building.

"I've got no idea," her daughter fretted. "Eli said to call when we got here…" She picked up her cellphone, and a minute later they saw Eli appear at the doors. He waved them over.

"They're only letting family in," he said, keeping his voice low. "So don't let them know you're not related. Grandpa's pretty shaken up, but he's dying to talk to you."

"David's coming, too," Moira told him. "Is that all right?"

Eli nodded. "Let me know when he gets here, and I'll come out to bring him in, too."

He led them through the two sets of doors, past a police officer who was assigned to guard the entrance, through the hallway where residents were congregated, muttering quietly to themselves, and past the dining room, which was where Moira paused. The dining room doors were propped open, and the interior was swarming with police officers. Someone from a forensics team was taking photo after photo of something. She could see what looked like a spray of blood across one of the white walls, and saw tape on the floor in the outline of a body.

"Come on," Eli said softly. "They want everyone to stay out of the way."

She followed him wordlessly the rest of the way to Reggie's room. Candice was silent beside her. *I've seen death before*, the deli owner thought. *But nothing quite so violent. What's going on here?*

Reggie, who was waiting for them in his room, heaved himself to his feet when they got there.

"Did Eli tell you what happened?" he asked, his eyes flashing with excitement.

"I didn't tell them the whole story yet, Gramps," the young man said. "David's on his way, too. Why don't we wait for him?"

"Nonsense. It's a good story, there's no harm in telling it twice."

"You don't have to sound so excited about it," Eli said, shaking his head. "A man died."

"A killer met with justice," Reggie declared, shaking his cane at his grandson. "Fine, I'll tell it if you don't want to. Take a seat, you two." This last part was directed at Moira and Candice, who obeyed, sitting down on the small loveseat next to the television.

"It all started when Eli and I were taking a stroll around the courtyard after dinner. I'm supposed to walk more, according to the nurses, though I still don't see why they seem to think the best time to do it is after I eat. No one wants to exercise when they're full. I guess they think they can tell me what to do just because I'm old, but really *I'm* paying their wages, *I* should be the one telling *them* to go and take a walk after dinner."

"Grandpa," Eli said gently. "The story, remember? I promised to talk to the nurses and get your walk moved to the morning, but I doubt that's what Moira and Candice want to hear about right now."

"Yes, well. Anyway, we were walking around that courtyard, talking about…" Here he shot a sly glance at Moira and gave a soft chuckle. "Well, I won't spoil it. Let's just say we were talking about some interesting personal matters, when out of the blue this guy starts shouting. It was Danny, of course. We could see him through the windows. He wanted to see the director, then started yelling for someone to call the police instead. He said something about the police questioning him about his mother's death, but by then the staff were trying to calm him down and it got hard to hear. He had a gun, though, I know that much. One of the nurses saw it under his jacket. I heard her shouting about it from all the way out in the courtyard. See, Eli? My hearing isn't bad. I don't need one of those electronic aids. I'm perfectly fine."

"That's only half of the story, gramps. We can talk about your hearing later. Do you want to finish it, or shall I?"

"I will. Quit being so impatient. You have to take time to tell a good story. Back to it, then." Reggie cleared his throat. "After a few minutes, a couple of the nurses managed to calm him down enough to convince him that he was scaring the residents. He agreed to wait in the dining room for the police, who were already on their way by then, and Nurse Southfield locked him in the second the doors shut behind him."

"So he was alone in a locked room?" Moira asked, confused. "Did he shoot himself?"

"That's the thing," Eli said, exchanging a look with Reggie. "No one heard a gunshot. When the police got here and unlocked the doors… he was dead."

The deli owner blinked, not understanding. "If he didn't shoot himself and he was alone… then how did he die?"

"Well, Nurse Southfield only locked the dining room doors," Eli said. "The door to the kitchen, which also has a door outside for deliveries and a door directly to the staff room, was still open.

Someone must have snuck in and killed him, then snuck back out before the police got there."

"Justice," Reggie said with satisfaction. "Someone must have been listening when I was telling everyone how he was a stinkin' murderer, and they decided to take matters into their own hands."

# CHAPTER FIFTEEN

By the time David got there, the four of them had already gone over the story a couple of times. Moira couldn't quite believe that one of the elderly residents of the nursing home had managed to stealthily and silently kill a man with a gun, but Reggie was convinced that that was what had happened.

"Griff always had a soft spot for Delilah," he said. "He brought her roses every week."

"Griff can barely walk," Moira pointed out. "He needs a walker just to walk in between tables in the dining room. How on earth would he have managed to kill someone, especially when that person was armed with a gun of their own?"

"He can walk better than he lets on," said Reggie huffily. "He just likes all of the attention he gets for needing help."

"Something about this just doesn't add up," said David once they had caught him up. "Why would Danny come back to Misty Pines after the police interviewed him? His flight was supposed to leave in less than a day. The smart thing to do would have been to lay low and wait for Thursday evening. What could he have to gain by confronting people here?"

Moira thought that the private investigator had a good point. Danny probably would have gotten away scot-free if he had just kept out of the way for the next day. She couldn't see why he had risked everything by coming back to the scene of his two murders... but wasn't it a well-known phenomenon that criminals tended to return to the scene of their crimes?

"Maybe he left behind some sort of evidence when he killed Beatrice or Delilah," she mused. "Something that would give the police a good enough reason to arrest him right away."

"Maybe." The private investigator still didn't look convinced.

"What are we going to tell the cops?" Reggie said suddenly. They all turned to look at him.

"What do you mean?" Eli asked. "If they talk to any of us for whatever reason, we'll just tell them the truth."

"But if I tell them that Griff was sweet on Delilah, then they might figure out he's probably the guy that killed Danny," the old man said. "Griff is a good guy; he doesn't deserve to go to jail."

"I'm sure other people knew about Griff and Delilah's relationship," Eli pointed out. "Besides, they aren't going to send a ninety-year-old man to prison. The best thing that we can do is give them all of the information that we have, and let them close this case as soon as possible. Until then, I can bet that security will be very tight."

"This whole thing is a mess," David said, shaking his head. "None of you should be involved in this in the first place. Reggie, if you think your friend Griff might have killed someone for *whatever* reason, then you must tell the police. Keeping that information from them won't help anybody. Eli, I understand why you were here, but you two…" He turned to look at Moira and Candice. "I have to ask, why on earth did you run *toward* a murder scene with a killer still on the loose?"

"It's not like we were in any danger," Moira said huffily. "There are police everywhere here, and Reggie wanted to see us. We've all been investigating the murders together, after all."

"Did you ever think that maybe you might be suspects?" he asked, raising an eyebrow. The deli owner froze.

"What do you mean?" she asked.

"Well, everyone here knows that you and I, along with Reggie, suspected Danny of killing his mother and aunt. And I'm sure Reggie let slip to some of his friends that Danny had a flight out of the country soon." The elderly man nodded. "So think of how it will look to the police when Danny mysteriously dies the day before his flight leaves, and you show up shortly after, Moira. I wouldn't be surprised if you and Reggie were the primary suspects."

The deli owner blanched. "They wouldn't really think that we killed him, would they?"

"Well, you do have something of a history of getting yourself into trouble down at the station." David massaged his temples. "I'm sure I can convince them that the two of you are innocent, since Reggie was out in the courtyard with witnesses when Danny was locked in the dining room… Moira, were you at the deli by any chance when you got the call?"

"No…" She realized what he was getting at and added, "I was at the candy shop. Candice has security cameras too, remember? I'm sure there's footage of us being in the building before Danny was killed."

"Good. I don't think you'll have any trouble this time, but it's probably a good idea for *both* of you to lay low for a while." He looked back and forth between Moira and Reggie. "Danny is dead, so we don't have to worry about him getting on that plane and flying away anymore. But any more poking around might get one or both of you into serious trouble. There have been three murders here in the past two and a half weeks. Trust me when I say tempers are going to be running *very* high at the police station for a while."

The conversation with David was sobering. Moira had been so involved with helping Reggie figure out who had killed his friends and trying to make up for not believing him right away that she hadn't paused to think how this would reflect on her. She had been a murder suspect before, and it was by no means a position that she wanted to find herself in again.

*At least Danny won't get away with killing his two family members,* she thought. *The only question is… who killed him?* She and Reggie might be the obvious suspects to outsiders, but *she* knew that neither of them had done it. Was Reggie right? Had Griff taken it in his own hands to kill the man who murdered the woman he loved? It made sense, sort of, until she remembered how frail he had looked the other day. Even if Reggie was right and his friend was fitter than he looked, that still didn't explain how he had managed to take down an armed man silently, on his own.

It was an unsatisfying ending to the twin mysteries of Beatrice's and Delilah's deaths, but it was an ending all the same. She had to accept that. She knew it drove David crazy when she dove headfirst into tracking down a killer, and she could see his point. She was lucky that she hadn't either been arrested or killed before now… and maybe it was time to stop pushing that luck.

# CHAPTER SIXTEEN

With Danny out of the picture, albeit more gruesomely than she would have liked, Moira was free to stop worrying about the murders and Danny's impending flight to freedom. Instead she could concentrate on other important matters, like her date with David on Friday night.

Things were finally beginning to calm down at the deli; they had stopped giving out the free samples of breakfast cookies, so the morning rush wasn't as crazy as it had been, and Dante had offered to pick up more morning hours again. She was finally beginning to feel settled enough to think about planning a fun trip or getaway with David. Her aborted conversation with Candice a few days ago had made her realize how important the private investigator really was to her. If she wanted a future with him, she couldn't let work get in the way.

To her surprise, she found herself getting nervous Friday evening as she was preparing for their date. She realized that it had been a long time since just the two of them had gone out together, and she was looking forward to it more than ever.

Deciding to go all out and dress up for an evening out, she pulled her new dress with the white rose trim out of her closet and tugged it on. It fit her just as well now as it had in the store the week before. She turned, admiring her reflection in the mirror. *Not too bad for someone halfway through her forties,* she thought, running her hands down the front of the dress to smooth away the wrinkles. *The tan helps, though it's already fading.*

"What do you think?" she said aloud to Diamond. The little black-and-white dog was laying on Moira's bed, watching her alertly. When the deli owner looked over at her, she began wagging her tail rapidly. "I'll take that as a compliment."

The new dress was only part of her ensemble. She left her naturally curly hair down, hoping that the product that she used would be strong enough to fend off the frizzies as the night wore on. She tucked a lock of it behind one of her ears to make sure her diamond earrings went well with the outfit, then gave her reflection her most winning smile.

She kept her makeup simple, using it to accentuate her natural features and hide some of the more annoying wrinkles. *That's one thing that all of the sun I got on the cruise didn't help with,* she thought as she squinted at her crow's feet. *I need to buy the good moisturizer again.*

A few minutes before David was supposed to pick her up she decided that she had done all that she could… and that she looked pretty good after all was said and done. She pulled on a pair of her trusty black pumps—nothing too high, it would be embarrassing to trip over herself—and grabbed her purse to wait by the door. The three dogs gathered around her, all of them watching expectantly out of the window. By now all of them, even Diamond who only spent a few days each month at her house, knew that her behavior meant that David was soon to arrive. Sure enough, he pulled up the driveway just as her phone's clock said it was eight-thirty. With butterflies in her stomach, the deli owner gave each of the dogs a quick pat goodbye, reminded them to behave themselves while she was gone, and slipped out the door.

"You look perfect," David said. He had gotten out of the car and had the passenger side door open for her. She paused for a quick kiss, then slid into the vehicle. The private investigator walked back around to his side and got in.

As he put the car into gear, Moira said, "You look pretty handsome yourself."

It was true. He seemed to have gone the extra step for this date himself: he was wearing a well-fitted black suit, his hair had been styled back, and he smelled of her favorite cologne.

"Only the best for you," he said with a smile.

The Redwood Grill was as busy as they'd ever seen it, but they didn't have to wait even a minute for their table. The hostess walked them back, leaving them with their menus and promising to have their drinks out soon.

"Denise runs a tight ship," Moira said, impressed. Every other table in the restaurant was packed, and she was surprised that they hadn't had to wait a few minutes, even with their reservation.

"She definitely goes the extra mile," David said, just as a chilled bottle of champagne along with two flutes were delivered to their table.

"Oh, but we didn't order—" Moira began.

"On the house," the waiter said, winking at her.

"What's wrong?" David asked after the waiter had gone.

"Oh, I'm just trying to remember if Denise owes me for anything," the deli owner said. "She made sure our table was free right away even though she's slammed tonight, she sent the champagne… and

133

look, isn't this one of her fancy tablecloths?" She plucked at the shimmering white cloth.

"Maybe she's just being a good friend?" he suggested, taking her hand.

"Oh, she's a great friend," Moira said. "She just usually isn't this *nice*."

"Not every mystery needs to be solved," David said with a chuckle. "Let's decide what we're eating. It looks like they changed the menus again."

Indeed they had, and the promise of trying a new entree distracted her from wondering what had gotten into Denise.

"Oh my goodness, it's going to be hard to choose," she said after perusing the menu. "What do you think you're going to get?"

"Mmm? Oh, probably just steak and potatoes," he said. "What about you?"

"I'm thinking about the pasta with lamb ragu," she told him. "It looks delicious."

He smiled over at her, and she noticed that he hadn't even opened his menu.

"Don't you want to see what their new dishes are?" she asked. "They've got some sort of shepherd's pie… it looks like something you'd like."

"I'm not feeling super hungry right now," he admitted. "I'd better stick to the basics. Besides, you can't go wrong with a good steak."

"David, are you feeling all right?" she asked him. On closer inspection, he did look slightly odd. His hand was shaking a bit, and he looked a shade paler than normal.

"I'm fine," he promised her. "I'm exactly where I want to be."

"All right…" Before she could say anything else, her phone buzzed from inside her purse. "It's Reggie," she said as she pulled it out. She shot David a quick glance, not wanting to be rude, but also curious to know what the elderly man could possibly want this late in the evening.

"Go ahead," he said with a smile. "I know if you don't answer it, you're going to be fretting about it all during dinner. I'm just as interested as you are to find out why he's calling right now."

"I'll keep it short," she promised. She hit the button to answer the call.

"Reggie, it's me. Is everything all right?"

"Moira," the old man said in a low voice. "You need to get over here right now. Bring David. I know who killed Beatrice and Delilah, and it wasn't Danny."

"What?" she asked, her own voice low and urgent. "What do you mean? What's going on?"

"She'll be back any minute," he said. "You've got to hurry… I think she killed Danny too."

"Reggie, what—" But it was too late; he had hung up.

Moira glanced up at David, her heart pounding. "We have to go, now."

"What do you mean?" he asked, frowning.

"Reggie is in trouble," she told him. "He thinks that someone other than Danny killed those two women… and from what I gathered, she might be on to him."

David spared one regretful look at the champagne, then turned to her with a look of resolve. "Let's go," he said. "I'll drive; you phone the police."

PATTI BENNING

# CHAPTER SEVENTEEN

"They said they're going to send a unit out immediately," Moira told David. She turned off her phone's screen and leaned her head back against the seat's headrest with a sigh of relief. "Are we almost there?"

David didn't answer. His grip on the wheel was so tight that his knuckles were white.

"David?" she said, then paused, her eyes searching the dark forest rushing by. She had been distracted by her phone call to the police when they pulled out of the Redwood Grill's parking lot, and hadn't been paying attention to the turns that they had been taking. Was it possible…? "David, are we going to my house?"

He nodded, still not speaking or meeting her gaze.

"What?" She sat bolt upright. "Reggie needs us! We have to go to Misty Pines."

"I'm not putting you into danger, Moira," he said. "I can't just drive you into a confrontation with a killer and a whole squad of police. I'm going to drop you off at your house, then go and see what I can do to help."

"But…" She trailed off. Arguing would be of no use. She saw the determination in his face, and had known him long enough to be able to tell when he had made an unshakable decision.

*Reggie,* she thought. *I'm sorry…*

He pulled up to her house and left his car running as he walked her to her door. "I'll come in for just a second. I want to make a call."

Without speaking to him she unlocked her front door and sat angrily on the couch while he pulled out his cellphone and walked into the other room. She wasted only a few seconds feeling helpless and angry when she decided that it wasn't helping anything. Getting up, she gestured the dogs to lie down and stay, then tiptoed out of the living room and down the hall to the kitchen. She paused at the doorway, listening to David's voice inside.

"You really can't do anything, Detective?" he said, sounding pretty upset himself. "I know this man. If he says he knows who Danny's killer is, chances are he does."

He ground his teeth, listening to the person on the other end of the phone.

"No! You can't just leave," he said after a moment. "What do you think is going to happen to him if he's right? Jefferson…"

Moira backed away. She had heard enough. It sounded like the police had gone to Misty Pines, but whatever Reggie told them hadn't been enough for them to make an arrest. *They don't believe him*, she thought angrily. *But I do, and I'm not letting the Misty Pines killer claim another victim.*

Casting an apologetic glance back at the kitchen door—David was going to be furious when he got off the phone and came out to find her gone—she grabbed her keys and purse off of the end table. If he wouldn't drive her to Misty Pines, then she was just going to have to drive herself.

She was halfway to the retirement home when she realized that she didn't know the code to get through the doors. She turned her phone's screen on to call Eli, and winced when she saw how many missed calls and texts from David she had. She had silenced her phone after the first call had come in, and that had turned out to be a smart move. She knew he was probably freaking out, but Reggie's life could very well be in danger. She had to save him, even if David never forgave her for what she was putting him through.

Luckily, Eli answered the phone and gave her the code before asking what was going on. She gave him a quick explanation as she drove, and was relieved when he promised to meet her there. Just because she was rushing headfirst into danger didn't mean she had a death wish, and there would definitely be safety in numbers.

She got to the assisted-living home before Eli did, though, and knew that she couldn't risk waiting around for him. Rushing through the first set of doors, she punched in the code for the second set and held her breath until the light turned green. She shoved the doors open and walked as quickly down the hall as she dared to without attracting unwanted attention to herself. Any one of the staff, or even the residents, could be the killer. It seemed to take her forever to reach Reggie's room. When he answered her knock on the first try, she felt a flood of relief wash through her.

"I'm so glad you're okay," she said when he opened the door. He hurried her inside and shut the door behind her, replacing the rubber doorstop. She was glad he still had it, even though she was sure the assisted-living home wouldn't like it.

"She hasn't come back since the police came," he told her in a low voice once the door was firmly shut. "It's just a matter of time, though. Where's David?"

She told him what happened, how David had driven her back home and called the police to see what they had found.

"They didn't believe me," Reggie said, settling into his armchair with a sigh. He looked exhausted. "I should have known—what did

I really expect to happen when I told them Alberta Radisson was the culprit?"

"The director?" Moira squeaked, utterly shocked.

Reggie nodded. "I didn't connect the dots until I went to go ask Griff if he was really the one that had killed Danny. He didn't know what I was talking about, so I spent about an hour after dessert explaining everything to him."

"And he told you Alberta did it?" she asked.

"No, no, he has no idea. What he told me was all about Delilah, and her will. Apparently just a couple of weeks before she died, she made Mrs. Radisson the sole benefactor of her estate," he said.

"Wow," Moira breathed, the pieces beginning to fly together rapidly. It all made sense. Alberta must have learned that Beatrice was planning on leaving everything to her sister when she passed. Moira had gathered that both sisters were quite wealthy—you pretty much had to be to live in a place like this. When Delilah put the director in her will, that made it so Alberta stood to inherit everything from both sisters… as long as Beatrice died first.

"She must have killed Beatrice to make sure her sister would inherit everything," the deli owner said, thinking out loud. "If she waited too long and Delilah died first, then she would have only gotten half of the fortune. If she killed them both, that means that she must have killed Danny too—I bet he was getting too close to the truth. He might have even planned to kill *her* out of revenge when he came in here with that gun."

Reggie nodded. "I figured all of that out, too."

"Wait, when you called me, you said that she was going to be back soon. Reggie... did you confront her about all of this?"

"No..." He hesitated, looking away from her. "I... ah... I tested my theory. I told her that Eli and I had gotten into a fight, and I wanted him out of my will, but I wasn't sure who else to leave my money to. The second I told her how much money I was leaving, she practically leapt onto the computer to print out the right forms. She promised to run them in to my lawyer first thing in the morning. Then I told her I was having second thoughts, and she practically begged me to sign."

"Even if she wasn't a killer, that's pretty disgusting behavior for the director of an assisted-living home," the deli owner said. "I bet she could lose her license over it."

"Oh, she'd get fired the moment word got out," Reggie said. "I told her I needed to sleep on it, then in the morning I was going to tell her that Eli and I had made up... and that's when the police came. They started questioning her after talking to me, and I was certain that she was going to jail. I don't know what she said to convince them that she was innocent, but they left and I've been locked in here ever since. Now that she knows I'm onto her, it's only a matter of time before she comes to add me to her list of kills."

"We need to get you out of here, Reggie," she said. "David and Eli are both on their way, but neither of them know any of this. When they come rushing in looking for us, the first person they talk to is bound to be…"

"The director," Reggie finished, paling. "She'll send them away, and come and find us herself."

Moira wasted a few minutes searching Reggie's room for anything that could be used as a weapon, but besides his cane—which he needed to walk—there was nothing. She decided they would just have to try their best not to be seen, and hope to make it to her SUV before the director realized that Reggie was missing.

She cracked the door to his room open and peeked down the hallway both ways cautiously. She didn't see anyone, not even a nurse, so she silently gestured to Reggie to follow her. Going was slow; the old man was exhausted, and could only walk at half his normal pace. Moira itched for a wheelchair so she could push him, but didn't see any that weren't in use.

The few residents that they passed didn't seem to think anything was amiss. The deli owner smiled and nodded at them, and offered Reggie her arm for balance. She was beginning to think that they were going to make it out of the building without being stopped when they rounded the corner and came face to face with Alberta.

The director looked nearly as shocked to see them as they were to see her, but she recovered more quickly. Moira could see the other woman's eyes dart between them, and recognized the exact moment she realized that her cover was blown.

"Moira Darling, how nice to see you," Alberta said, her voice sickeningly sweet. "It's a bit later than we usually allow non-family members to visit, but I'll let it slide if you come with me."

"Actually, we were just on our way out for a breath of fresh air," the deli owner replied, forcing a smile of her own. "We won't be long, I promise."

A pair of nurses escorting an unsteady older woman was passing, and Moira gambled that the director wouldn't do anything out of character with them around.

"Oh, in that case to allow me to escort you out," the other woman said. "I wouldn't mind a chance to look at the stars myself."

The deli owner wondered what would happen if she began shouting accusations at the other woman, but, as if she could read her mind, Alberta shifted at that instant and Moira saw the glint of a knife tucked into her waistband. Gritting her teeth, Moira nodded and began walking with Reggie at her side. No one stopped them.

They had just reached the front entranceway when the doors swung open. David and Eli walked in, the worry on their faces draining away when they saw Moira and Reggie standing with the director.

"I'm so glad you're both safe," David groaned. "You just about gave me a heart attack when you drove away like that, Moira."

Moira held his gaze and widened her eyes, tilting her head toward the director. The private investigator frowned and raised an eyebrow. She bit her lip in frustration.

"I'd like to talk to Moira and Reggie in private," the director said calmly. "They've both been causing a fair bit of trouble around here lately."

"Of course," Eli said. "It won't take long, will it? We need to have a chat, too."

"Just a few minutes," the director replied with a smile. "Ms. Darling, Reginald, would you please follow me into my office?"

Moira didn't move. Her gaze was still locked with David's willing him to understand her. She tilted her head toward the director again, widened her eyes, and slowly shook her head.

David frowned. She could tell he was beginning to get it.

"I don't have all night," Alberta said sharply. Moira glanced over and paled to see that her right hand was under her frock, right where the hilt of her knife would be. David was still hesitating, and they were running out of time. At any moment, the director could snap and kill any of them.

"Okay," David said suddenly. Moira jumped and turned back to look at him. She wasn't sure if he was talking to her or Alberta. "I'm just so glad you're all right. You were in such a hurry to get over here; I was afraid that you had crashed somewhere. I've got to hug you before I let you out of my sight again."

Alberta was glaring at them, but didn't say anything as David approached and wrapped his arms around her.

"It's her," Moira whispered, her lips against his ear. "She killed all three of them, and she has a knife."

"Are you sure?" he asked, brushing a kiss across her cheek.

She nodded, hoping that he would trust her without more questions. He pulled away.

"Eli and I will just take a seat in the dining room, if that's okay," he said calmly, facing Alberta. She hesitated for a fraction of a second, then nodded.

David gestured to Eli, who was looking very confused, to follow, then walked toward the dining room doors. To get to them, he had to pass by Alberta. When he was a step past her, he spun on his heel and grabbed her by the arm, twisting her hand away from the knife and forcing her to her knees at the same time. She screeched at him to let go, but he was strong enough that she couldn't squirm out of his grip.

"Eli, check her belt," he said. "There should be a knife."

By now a crowd had gathered to watch them. Eli, who looked frightened but determined, did as David said. When he withdrew the large, bloodstained kitchen knife, the people gathered around gasped.

"I'm guessing that's the knife that was used to kill Danny," David said grimly as he pulled a pair of handcuffs out of his jacket and snapped them on to Alberta's wrists. "Planning to pin that murder on Moira?" He shook his head. "Someone call the police and tell them we have the person responsible for all three deaths restrained and waiting for them."

# CHAPTER EIGHTEEN

Watching the police arrest Alberta and formally apologize to Reggie put Moira in an ebullient mood. Not only had they caught the killer, but Reggie was now the local hero of Misty Pines. Even David was in a good mood, despite her diving headfirst into danger yet again.

"We make a good team," he said with a grin. They were sitting in the common area at the assisted-living home, waiting around for the police to finish questioning the others.

"Yeah, we do," the deli owner agreed. "I'm glad you trusted me. For a second there, I thought you didn't believe me."

"I'll always believe you when it counts," he said. "I'd never forgive myself if I didn't and something happened to you."

"I'm sorry for taking off like that. I felt terrible for doing it, but I heard you talking to the police, and I just couldn't leave Reggie here alone with no help."

"I was worried about you… very worried," he admitted. "But you made the right call. He's lucky to have a friend like you."

They both looked over at Reggie, who was still talking animatedly to one of the police officers. He was leaning heavily on his cane, but still seemed to have plenty of energy for the retelling of his story. Eli was just finishing up talking to a detective, and they waved him over when he was done.

"I want to thank you—again—Moira," he said. "I can't wait to tell Candice everything. She's going to be so upset that I didn't wake her up for it."

"I bet," the deli owner said with a laugh. "She doesn't like to be left out of anything, especially not rescue missions."

"How did your dinner go?" Eli asked suddenly, as if remembering something. He glanced at Moira, then looked to David with furrowed brows.

"We didn't get a chance to finish it," the private investigator explained. "Reggie called partway through."

"Ah." Eli grimaced. "Sorry, man. Well, I'm not sorry that you rushed over here and saved my grandfather, but sorry that you had to cut things short. There will be another day."

"Yeah." David looked at Moira, his gaze warm. She raised an eyebrow, and he grinned.

"I think we're going to take a walk, Eli," he said. "Say goodnight to Reggie for us." And before the deli owner could object, he had grabbed her hand and was tugging her past the police officers, through the doors, and out into the chilly night.

"What was all of that about?" Moira asked as they walked along the tree line. It was quiet outside compared to the hubbub inside, and she felt peaceful.

"There's something I need to do," he said. He turned and put a hand gently on her arm to stop her. She watched him fumble in his jacket pocket, then took a shocked step backwards as he got down on one knee.

"Moira Darling," he began. "You drive me crazy—crazier than anyone I've ever known. But that's because I love you more than anyone I've ever known. I can't imagine spending my life with anyone but you. Will you marry me?"

She gasped as he opened a small black box to reveal a gorgeous, intricate diamond ring. Her hands went to her mouth and she felt tears come to her eyes.

"Yes," she whispered. He broke into an ear-to-ear grin and slid the ring onto her waiting finger.

It fit perfectly. Something tickled the back of her mind, a memory from a few weeks ago...

"Wait. After that time you and Maverick were upstairs, I found one of my favorite rings that had been lost since I got back from the cruise," she said, the gears turning in her head. "Did you take it?"

"Ah... yeah. I did." He gave her a sheepish look. "I needed to make sure the ring was the right size, so I took that ring to a jeweler while you were gone. I forgot to put it back until that night. I had hoped that you hadn't noticed."

"You must have been planning this for a while," she said, amazed. She couldn't stop looking at her engagement ring and smiling. It didn't feel real yet... she and David were going to get married.

"Over a month," he admitted. "I've been waiting for the perfect moment to propose. This," he gestured around the dark woods and the parking lot, "isn't exactly what I had in mind, but I couldn't bear waiting any longer. I wanted to do it over a nice candlelit dinner."

"Oh, David, this is perfect," she told him. "Just you and me under the stars. I can't think of a better moment."

"I'm glad you're happy." He pulled her close for a tender kiss, then wrapped his arms around her and rested his forehead against hers. "I'm glad you said yes. I was terrified that you wouldn't."

"Why on earth wouldn't I want to marry you?" she asked him.

"That's what all of your friends said," he told her with a chuckle.

"You asked them before you asked me?" she grumbled, recalling the strange behavior of her friends and employees over the past few weeks.

"Well, I didn't know if you wanted to marry again, after everything that happened with Mike, and I didn't want to put pressure on you if it wasn't something you were interested in. I only brought it up with Candice, Martha, and Denise, but it turns out they're all terrible at keeping secrets. I'm pretty sure half the town knew I was going to propose to you. I'm surprised that you *didn't* know."

"They managed to keep it a secret from me, just like that surprise party," she assured him. "I'm floored. This is the best night of my life. David, I'm so happy I don't even have words for it."

"You don't need words."

He tilted her head up and kissed her again, and Moira realized that he was right. She didn't need to say anything. Everything that she wanted to tell him, she could feel in the tender way that he held her, and in the pounding of her heart as they kissed. No words could ever describe this moment. She wished it could last forever.

Made in the USA
San Bernardino, CA
11 September 2016